THE ANCHOR CLANKERS

Renee Garrison

Published by:
Southern Yellow Pine (SYP) Publishing
4351 Natural Bridge Rd.
Tallahassee, FL 32305

www.syppublishing.com

This is a work of fiction. Names, characters, places, and events that occur either are the products of the author's imagination or are used fictitiously. Any resemblance to actual persons, places, or events is purely coincidental.

The contents and opinions expressed in this book do not necessarily reflect the views and opinions of Southern Yellow Pine Publishing, nor does the mention of brands or trade names constitute endorsement.

ISBN-10: 1-59616-053-5
ISBN-13: 978-1-59616-053-8
ISBN-13: ePub 978-1-59616-054-5
ISBN-13: Adobe eBook 978-1-59616-055-2
Library of Congress Control Number: 2017943297

Printed in the United States of America
First Edition
May 2017

For my parents

Acknowledgements

I'm grateful to those who helped me write this book, particularly the alumni of the Sanford Naval Academy for sharing their lives and laughter. My memory needed jogging and you inspired me.

Fred Thomas, my creative mentor at *The Tampa Tribune*, who once described my writing style as "delightfully bitchy."

Carl Lennertz, a publishing veteran who found the Anchor Clankers' story as engaging as I did, and persuaded me to rewrite it.

Liz Sims, an extraordinary editor (and a better friend) with an amazing grasp of the adolescent mind and vocabulary.

And of course, thank you Terri Gerrell for all you do.

Finally, to my family, especially my husband (whose opinion matters the most.) Despite our financial crisis, you gave me a thesaurus and urged me to, "Keep writing." Your encouragement remains the best Christmas gift I've ever received.

PROLOGUE

She swung her legs over the side of the boat and slipped into the water.

"Hold the rope with two hands, both palms facing down and the rope between the tips of your skis."

Easier said than done, she thought. Things floated in different directions in the water.

"This boat goes from zero-to-fast speed, but that helps you get up on the skis."

Now Suzette was really nervous.

"Keep your arms out straight," the boys in the boat hollered.

Suzette lurched forward over the skis and hit the water face first. Her lifejacket lodged up around her ears, taking her bikini top with it. She tried to pull them both down quickly when she noticed her skis floating upside-down in the water.

The boat circled around and came alongside her.

"Next time, let the lifejacket keep you floating on top of the water and try leaning back."

Suzette nodded and tried shoving her left foot into a ski while preventing the right one from drifting beyond her reach. When the boat accelerated, she held on as long as she could—until her skis careened in opposite directions and the rope slipped out of her hands.

"Let the boat pull you out of the water and up onto your skis." The boys were laughing at her, now. "If you bend your arms or pull yourself up out of the water, you'll lose your balance."

She flipped over from her stomach onto her back and struggled to get two skis pointing skyward. Her feet drifted apart. Whenever they got close together, the skis crossed over each other. Even the smallest wave seemed to push her legs out of control.

"There can't be any slack in the rope when the boat starts going or else it will jerk you forward and cause you to fall," someone shouted. "Once the rope is tight in your hands, let the boat move forward slowly and drag you for a minute before we hit the gas."

Suzette pulled a handful of wet hair back from her face and attempted to pull her knees up close to her chest. She held onto the rope as she was dragged along behind the boat. She heard the word, "Ready?" Then suddenly she was almost airborne, semi-standing, until one ski skidded over the boat wake. At full speed, she landed in a perfect split, forcing her bikini bottom into the most painful wedgie she had ever experienced.

"If you try to cross the wake with one ski at a time, you'll fall," one boy said, shaking his head. "Make sure you cross at a sharp angle with both skis at the same time. If you go slowly, you'll fall."

"No kidding."

Being a Florida girl was a lot tougher than it looked.

"Lesson's over," she gasped as she pushed her skis toward the boat ladder. Suzette wasn't sure she had enough strength to climb aboard. Someone reached down and grabbed her arm above the elbow, hoisting her into the boat. She wrapped herself in a beach towel and eased into a seat.

"Just remember to keep your knees bent while you're trying to get up," a midshipman said as he pulled the tow rope in and carefully looped it so it wouldn't tangle. "That helps you balance and control your skis better."

Suzette considered hitting his bronzed chest with those skis, but her arms felt as limp as boiled spaghetti.

CHAPTER 1
Arrival in Hell

Suzette never had a brother—at least not a biological one—until she acquired over a hundred of them as a freshman in a new high school in Florida.

Sunshine and boys may sound like a teen-aged girl's dream—maybe if the girl had a choice.

While her older sister got to stay up north in college, Suzette's parents dragged her away from all she knew to start a new life, not of her choosing.

After twenty-eight years in the Navy, her father retired and accepted a position as Commandant of the Sanford Naval Academy which sounded important but was just a fancy name for a private school. The campus dominated the southern shore of Lake Monroe in the dead center of Florida. Heat and humidity hung in the air, making everything feel as sticky as the bathroom after you showered. Like many new residents of the state, Suzette learned quickly not to spend much time outside on summer evenings or risk the mosquitoes, gnats, and an alien species called "no-see-ums" eating her alive.

So, this is Florida? she thought.

She looked down at the jeans she wore to keep from freezing in the air-conditioned airport, which now stuck to her legs like wet laundry. Her dog, Skipper, lay panting on the seat beside her. Just hauling her suitcase from the trunk of the car to the motel room worked up a sheen of sweat.

Suzette could barely stay awake during the drive on Interstate 4. Tall cranes hovered over construction of nearby Walt

Disney World, but cows grazed in the fields oblivious, with tiny white birds hopping beside them. Central Florida definitely didn't resemble the brief snippet of a "Spring Break" movie her best friend's brother had rented on the sly. Her friend wanted to watch more, but Suzette was trained to be a good Catholic girl.

The Captain steered their Chevrolet Impala onto a two-lane road that curved along the shore of Lake Monroe. To the right, Suzette noticed a thicket of palmetto underbrush covered in a tangle of vines.

"It looks like a scene from a Tarzan movie," she said. "Probably the perfect breeding ground for snakes and God-knows-what."

To her left, blue water stretched far into the distance in search of the opposite shore.

Must be a pretty big lake, she thought, because the water looked flat, almost fake.

Suzette already missed her friends, Maine lobster rolls, and the hoodie she slipped into when the sun set and the breezes picked up on Cape Cod. She'd probably never wear a sweatshirt in this place.

The car passed a dilapidated house with a tin roof. Suzette strained to see if the locals looked like the "Beverly Hillbillies."

Mercifully, the Captain pulled into the parking lot of the only hotel in Sanford and as Suzette referred to it, "the scene of the crime."

"You heard about this job when you were sitting in the bar, here?" she asked.

"Yes, I met a gentleman in the cocktail lounge who told me the academy had an open position," he answered, sounding annoyed. "His son goes to school, there."

As soon as her father unlocked the hotel room door, her mother turned the thermostat down as low as it would go.

5

"Thank God for air conditioning," she murmured.

Suzette shimmied out of her jeans and crawled under the cool, white sheets. In minutes, she was sound asleep.

The next day, Suzette chose a sundress to wear to lunch.

Her mom suggested "lady-like attire" for this meet-and-greet with the current superintendent of the academy. She even bought a strapless bra for Suzette to wear under the lightweight dress "for modesty's sake." Ironically, Suzette noticed the bra's molded cups gave her more womanly curves. She couldn't see why it would matter if she and her mother walked in with one eye in the middle of their foreheads. The school hired the Captain, not his family.

Her father was chatty on the way over.

"The academy has been around since 1963," he offered. "The Bernard MacFadden Foundation established it in an old resort hotel complex called the Mayfair Inn. The school overlooks the lake."

"When will I see my school?" Suzette was already warm on the sunny side of the car, and she wanted to see where she would be going to school for the next four years, not the boys' academy.

Her mother replied, "Later, sweetie. You're going to love it."

"I'm sure," Suzette said under her breath, staring out at the flat, sandy landscape. She saw run-down buildings beside the highway, their signs fading in the sun, and fought the urge to cry.

CHAPTER 2
Welcome Aboard

Suzette looked at the school brochures. According to the literature, private boarding schools—with their small class size, structured environment, and twenty-four-hour supervision—were the primary vehicle for raising young gentlemen to embody the values of integrity, honor, duty, and service to others.

The Sanford Naval Academy utilized a military structure to achieve that mission.

The routine of class, physical activity, military training, and study varied little from day to day. Midshipmen were responsible for the cleanliness of their rooms, for shining their shoes, and for taking care of their uniforms. For many, these were alien activities prior to arriving at the school.

"They're called midshipmen?" Suzette asked.

"Yes indeed, because this is a naval academy," the Captain replied. "If this were the army, the boys would be called cadets. I just hope they're…"

He paused in mid-sentence.

"Well, I've heard of boarding schools that function as a kind of warehouse for children with academic or legal problems, or simply those unfortunate enough to be a hindrance to the travel agendas of their wealthy, divorced parents, but I'm sure this place isn't like that."

A white stucco building with a red barrel-tile roof, the academy stood like an aging matron in need of a makeover. As the car drove slowly along the long side of the building, Suzette noticed three boys sitting on a wooden bench outside what looked to be a kitchen entrance. Wearing striped uniform pants and white T-shirts, they blew smoke rings into the air and laughed uncontrollably. They looked her age, but it was hard to tell since short, military haircuts made everyone look six years old. She wondered what was so funny, but it would be years before she understood they were getting stoned on school property.

The Captain parked in front of the school where a blue-and-gold crest emblazoned a covered entryway. The place reminded Suzette a little of photographs of the luxurious resort, The Breakers, in Palm Beach, which she had seen in magazines. She looked at the cobwebs and guessed the similarities ended at the front door.

Her father pulled the car door open, and a wave of humid air struck Suzette in the face, fogging her glasses. Despite her bad vision, she pulled them off and dropped them on the back seat as she stood. What did she really need to see at this school, anyway? *Without my glasses, this place might look better,* she thought.

Superintendent Hugh Pointdexter stood at the top of the broad entry steps. Small in stature, Pointdexter had arrived from the Sidwell Friends School in Washington, DC. The Captain had no way of knowing that Pointdexter secured his position through family connections rather than any real expertise in running a private boarding school.

He greeted them enthusiastically, and his toothy smile reminded Suzette of a jack-o-lantern. His eyes crinkled into slits and practically disappeared.

"Welcome, welcome," he grinned. "Let me show you around."

The lobby was huge, with clusters of stuffed chairs, hallways leading every which way, and a grand staircase.

8

Pointdexter explained: "Administrative offices and your living quarters are downstairs. The midshipmen live upstairs."

He led them down a long hallway with creaky, wooden floors. Impossibly high ceilings and glass transoms above each door harkened back to the days before air conditioning. The air had a musty odor that tickled the inside of Suzette's nose until she sneezed.

At the end of the corridor, Pointdexter opened doors into a large dining hall with long, long tables. Metal chairs and eating utensils clattered above the noise of students who were enrolled in summer school. As Pointdexter pulled out her mother's chair, the decibel level dropped to mere whispers. Eyes watched, unsure of the group's purpose.

Black women emerged in kitchen aprons carrying trays of food—a luxury not enjoyed by the students who went through the cafeteria line, Suzette noticed. As a heaping bowl of mashed potatoes was placed in front of her, Suzette felt slightly uncomfortable, like she'd been dropped into a scene from the movie, "Gone with the Wind." Another enormous bowl of something Pointdexter identified as fried okra appeared next, along with a platter of pork tenderloin with gravy.

"Your family can dine here with the midshipmen whenever you like," Pointdexter said with his toothy grin.

Like that will ever happen, Suzette thought, as she tentatively took a bite of okra. It tasted crunchy on the outside—like a tater tot—but slimy on the inside. Ugh. She was feeling a little slimy herself, as the only teenage girl in a room full of boys in military uniforms. Suzette understood their curiosity, although she couldn't read any of their faces without her glasses. Obviously, the blonde wearing the dress wasn't a prospective student, more like something on a specimen slide in biology class.

9

Suzette was relieved when the meal mercifully ended and Pointdexter resumed his tour of the premises. They walked across the vast lobby and down another endless hallway with doors every ten feet. It was another testament to its original life as a hotel. The former guest rooms now functioned as administrative offices.

Pointdexter turned and smiled. "Your new home."

The group rounded a corner and stopped abruptly before another door. The "new home" turned out to be nothing more than a corridor of the old hotel that had been blocked off with the addition of a wall and an entry door. They entered the main living area, another hallway with a series of doors on either side that lead to bedrooms, a kitchen, and a laundry room. One former guestroom served as the formal living room.

"I guess I'll take this bedroom because it looks a little bigger than the other one directly across the hall," Suzette said.

It had a step up to the bathroom, a tall window overlooking the front portico of the school, and it looked like all of her furniture, arriving by truck soon, would fit in it. There were twin beds—one to sprawl on and one to sleep in—with a nightstand in between, a chest of drawers on one wall, and a long dresser with a mirror above it on the opposite one.

"Your sister's bed can go in the smaller room, but she won't care since she'll only visit during college breaks," her mother announced.

The same high ceilings she'd seen in the lobby loomed above the family's living quarters. Thank God for Willis Carrier, who invented air conditioning, or Suzette was certain she might die of heat exhaustion. Fortunately, air conditioning was installed in the building's first floor offices, classrooms, and the apartment. The boys who slept upstairs, she'd learn later, relied on portable fans

10

or cross ventilation in the corner rooms, which were reserved for seniors and officers.

Suzette decided the only bad thing about her room was its proximity to the front door of their living quarters. Her parents' bedroom was at the other end of the hallway, so she would become the doorman-by-default. Even worse, anyone standing at the door could stare directly into her room. Sure, there was a bedroom door, but when she closed it, the room got stuffy. If she left it open, she felt like a goldfish in a bowl.

"This is an awful old building," she said. "We might as well be living in a train car."

"Look, I know it's a big change, but I really need you to give the place a chance. Your dad has finally found a job, and we need to support him. Don't worry about it. Fresh paint and some new draperies will make this apartment feel homier. You'll see."

A wrecking ball would work better, Suzette thought. She didn't want to see any fresh paint. She wanted to go home, back to Boston where she belonged.

When the moving van left, the real work began. Suzette helped her mother set up the kitchen first. She figured a fork might come in handy later when she wanted to eat.

"We should probably give some of these glasses to Goodwill," Mom said, eyeing a former Welch's jelly jar-turned-juice-glass. "We can't possibly use all of them, and they take up so much cabinet space."

Suzette didn't see a dishwasher in the old hotel-room-turned-kitchen, just some space beside the sink for a wire drying rack. Fewer glasses meant less washing for her, so she nodded.

11

She was shoving so much packing paper into a trash bag—a noisy business—she almost didn't hear the knock at the apartment front door.

Opening it, she stared at two, pretty, blonde girls standing on the other side.

"I'm Debbie, and this is Janice. We're on the academy cheerleading squad, and Mr. Pointdexter told us the new Commandant had a daughter. We're having practice across the street in the gym and came over to see if you want to join us."

Mom walked up behind Suzette.

"That sounds like fun. Why don't you go?"

Suzette hesitated. She had known some of the cheerleaders at her middle school and envied them. They were cute and popular, but never very tall, so Suzette figured the sport wasn't an option for her. At five-foot-eight, she towered over the two girls standing in front of her. When she learned that Janice and Debbie were seniors, Suzette decided not to share the fact that she was a fourteen-year-old freshman. Her height helped her look older in the past, and she hoped it would kind of level the playing field with the cheerleaders.

They walked to the academy gymnasium, which stood by itself across the street. Laura explained that the academy held cheerleading tryouts every spring for local girls. Most of the girls attended Sanford High School and considered cheering for the Academy to be the perfect training regimen to make the varsity squad at their own school.

"Practice is held every Tuesday after school from four to six. Our squad has eight cheerleaders and two alternates. If you miss a practice, you have to sit out the next game. We'll give you patterns and fabric to sew your own uniform. We wear gold, pleated skirts with a really cute, navy blue sailor-top."

12

Not much of a surprise to Suzette since it was a naval academy.

It all sounded pretty simple, until she got to the gym.

Like Suzette, the girls were wearing T-shirts and shorts, no glamorous cheerleading outfits, and they were stretching on the shiny, wooden floor.

"Our goal is for everyone to be able to do a split by football season," Janice announced. "We've got to look good for the anchor clankers."

"Who?" Suzette was puzzled.

"Oh, that's what the local guys call the midshipmen," Janice said, laughing. "Just so y'all know, we cheer for the anchor clankers' team."

Suzette nodded and began to copy the moves, pointing her right toe and sliding one leg out in front of her while keeping the back leg straight and lowering herself to the floor.

She wasn't in bad shape, but the muscles in her left thigh throbbed just as her right knee screamed to stop this immediately.

"You'll get it," Debbie said, sitting beside Suzette on the floor. "It just takes practice. I didn't even make the squad at Sanford High the first time I tried out."

She decided to watch more and attempt less. Why hadn't she worn her glasses? The girls did a series of jumps, leaping high into the air, holding blue and gold pom-poms in each hand. Then came the endless routines with everyone except Suzette perfectly in sync.

After two hours, they were done.

"I hope you're not sore tonight," Janice said as she packed her shoes and water bottle into a gym bag. She looked a bit like a Barbie doll with expertly-applied makeup and impossibly thick eyelashes, the result of using a tube of mascara a week, no doubt. Suzette was in awe of the girl and doubted that she could ever look that good. The only thing on her own face was the Clearasil she dabbed over a few pimples.

She walked outside with the girls and watched as they headed to their cars. Like Janice and Debbie, most of the cheerleaders were seniors; a couple of them were juniors. She was the only freshman and couldn't even get a learner's permit for a year.

Limping back across the street, she hoped she would make it to the apartment. Her right thigh was exploding with muscle spasms while the other leg quivered slightly from over-exertion. They might not support her weight much longer.

"How was it?" Mom chirped, collapsing an empty cardboard box to the floor.

"A lot harder than it looks. If you need me, I'll be in the tub."

Suzette saluted her mom, and they both laughed.

CHAPTER 3
Asylum Harbor

S uzette watched a teabag bobbing in her cup as Mom surveyed the apartment. She sighed when her mother asked what she thought of it.

"Contrary to what you might think, this place really isn't so bad," Mom said.

Sure, their house on the Naval Air Station in New Orleans had been lovely with its large, fenced backyard, but that wasn't an option any more. Suzette liked living there, but when her father abruptly retired from the Navy, the family headed home to New England and moved in with Suzette's grandparents, temporarily. Nearly a year later, the Captain insisted on driving to Florida to look for a job.

"Would you still have married Dad if you had known how many times you'd have to move?" Suzette asked as she tore brown packing tape off a box of bed linens.

"Probably, because I was in love," Mom answered. "And it makes me kind of sad to think most of my childhood friends still live in the suburbs around Boston. They bought homes only blocks away from the houses where we grew up, and they spend every Sunday with their extended families. That's the kind of life I always wanted."

"So, what happened?"

"I guess I was flattered when a good-looking pilot started writing to me from flight school training in Pensacola," Mom recalled. "We met at a party. Dad came with a friend, and I thought his big brown eyes looked very intriguing."

Mom smiled. "Flying airplanes seemed like such a glamorous job compared to what the local boys had planned for their careers. I really didn't see myself marrying a plumber."

She shook her head. Once again, the Captain had gone to work, leaving his wife to settle the chaos of cardboard boxes in his wake. The pattern had been established long ago, twenty-three years to be exact.

"Your father started a new job at American Airlines in Rochester, New York, right before our wedding and left me to settle our first apartment—in a blizzard without a car," she said, shaking her head at the memory. Only twenty-one years old, she feared she might lose her mind out of sheer loneliness. Wadding up a pile of packing paper, she told her daughter about the day she pulled on a heavy coat, woolen scarf, and rubber boots to trudge several blocks in blowing snow to a diner. It was a desperate attempt for the young bride to have some human contact, but when she arrived, the restaurant was closed.

"As I look back, it seems pretty prophetic," she said with a sad smile.

The Captain was assigned to an aircraft carrier for six years of sea duty, but instead of living alone with her two daughters in Norfolk, Virginia, Suzette's mother returned to Massachusetts and rented an apartment close to her parents' home. Life there had some semblance of normalcy, even with an absentee father. Suzette and her sister loved their elementary school, and they spent every Sunday after church at their grandparents' house for dinner. The Captain flew home to visit one weekend each month until he received orders to Philadelphia followed by New Orleans.

Mom sighed.

"It's always been hard for me to watch you say goodbye to your friends and start over in new schools," she said softly.

"Hopefully, this will be our last move. At least your sister is enrolled in college, now. There's no more upheaval for her."

Suzette was tired of hearing her father complain about the cold weather back in Boston. When the job offer came, the family moved to Florida..., but a boarding school for boys?

Suzette could almost feel her mother's concern for her—worried about how her impressionable daughter would adjust to being around so many boys. It was kind of sweet, and knowing her mother was worried for her almost gave her strength. Something her grandfather used to say flashed in her mind: "You cannot discover new oceans unless you build enough courage to lose sight of the familiar shoreline."

This looked like it might be a trip on the Titanic.

The Captain seemed a little anxious as he brushed a speck of dust off his cap.

"Are you glad to be back in a uniform again?" Suzette asked, watching as he stood before a hallway mirror. Her father was about to meet his Battalion Staff. They had arrived at the school last night, a week before classes were scheduled to begin.

"Yes, but I'm not sure the midshipmen feel the same way," he answered. "I've been reviewing a list of twelve juniors and seniors who have been identified as leaders in the school: Battalion Commander, Executive Officer, Battalion Adjutant, two Commandant's Aides, one Headmaster's Aide, one Superintendent's Aide, two Petty Officers, a Supply Officer, Chief Petty Officer, and Staff Officer."

"The roster sounds legitimate, but what do I know?" he said. "I never had a son and never attended boarding school. I plan to treat these boys like any new recruits under my command."

17

"Compared to landing a jet on the flight deck of a moving aircraft carrier, how hard can a group of boys be?" Suzette asked, laughing. "Do you need help carrying stuff out to your office?"

He nodded, surprised by her offer. Actually, Suzette was curious to see the midshipmen, and holding a box of stuff for her father's desk seemed like a good excuse.

They walked out to the main lobby. Like other areas of the school, it had been given a nautical name: The Quarterdeck.

"Just drop that box in my office," the Captain said curtly.

He strode to a waiting group of boys and shook each hand as student leader and Battalion Commander Bill Moore introduced them. Suzette remembered hearing her father talk about his background. Though he was only seventeen, Moore had attended summer school to earn enough credits to graduate a year early. The Captain felt sure he would make a good ally.

Suzette dawdled in her father's office, watching as he smiled at the boys and patted several on the back. Then he began inspecting their uniforms.

"Mr. Russell, your shirt is frayed at the collar and sleeve," the Captain intoned. "In addition, the hem of your pants looks a tad short."

Battalion Adjutant Tim Russell was momentarily speechless.

"Sir, my apologies, sir."

"As one of my officers, I expect you to set an example for others," the Captain replied.

Suzette had heard enough. She guessed that if parents could afford the tuition at this place, they could probably afford a few new uniform shirts, too. No one noticed when she walked quietly back to the apartment and carried Skipper outside.

18

"Whoa. A real G.I. Joe, that guy," Tim Russell muttered quietly to Bill Moore as the Captain marched down the front portico steps.

Then he noticed the man speaking to a woman and a girl with white blonde hair that was almost as long as her tanned legs.

"Who are they?"

Bill glanced outside.

"They would be the Captain's wife and daughter," Bill answered.

The Captain got into his car, but the women lingered in the grass with a small silver Schnauzer. Tim headed towards them.

"That's not much of a dog," Tim said, coming down the front steps. "You must be Mrs. LeBlanc. Hi, I'm Tim Russell."

"Hey there; you look like a real sea dog," he said softly, bending to scratch the mascot's ears.

Suzette stared at him. The guy was a hunk. Streaked, blond hair and super tan, he must be a surfer or a water-skier, especially with that body. She could feel the sweat starting at the waistband of her shorts and trickling down the back of her thighs.

"Yes, and this is my daughter, Suzette," Mom answered. "The dog's name is Skipper."

Tim looked up from rubbing the dog's belly and squinted at the girl.

"You're obviously not going to school, here. Will you be at Sanford High School?"

Suzette was glad the sun was behind her. That way he couldn't see that her face was beet red from the heat—or because she was blushing. Not to mention, five new pimples were probably forming under the sweat.

"No, my parents chose a Catholic high school in Orlando. I'll be going there."

Of course, her education would occur elsewhere. She figured that people who send their sons to military school want structure and a strong male influence for their children.

They did not, however, want girls.

Tim nodded. "That's probably better for you. I'm not sure the guys at Sanford High would even speak to a girl who lives with the anchor clankers. In case you haven't heard, that's what they call us, here."

The public school in Sanford struggled with violence and teacher turnover, so her parents chose to send Suzette to a parochial high school forty-five minutes away.

When they visited the campus, she was given a copy of the "Student Handbook," which she assumed (incorrectly) had been printed decades ago. Why else would there be a reference to "white ankle socks and saddle shoes?"

"Miss LeBlanc, our students prefer ankle socks in the warm months and knee socks in the winter," the admissions counselor said primly, as she directed them to the uniform closet.

Suzette would rather wear chainmail.

"This is insane," she whispered to her mother. "'Our Lady of Perpetual Guilt' has an antiquated dress code in the ugliest shade of gray I've ever seen."

Suzette tried on a pleated skirt which hung, limply, from her waist to her knees like a broken accordion.

Ironically, it did make her feel a slight connection to the midshipmen. At least if she had to wear a uniform, it was comforting to know the midshipmen did, too. Her pleated skirt was the identical shade of gray as the uniform pants and shirts they wore. Suzette figured they were all prisoners, of sorts, living in a place they would not have chosen for themselves.

⚓

20

A narrow road stretched between the academy building and Lake Monroe. Suzette found a grassy strip between the road and the lake shore to walk her dog. She loved watching the seagulls, along with the occasional pelican dive-bombing for fish. Sometimes, she spotted a squall line sending gray sheets of rain across the lake. She wondered if boaters got caught in these pop-up storms, as she'd seen off Cape Cod.

Even on the hottest days, cats' paws—the light breezes that ruffle small areas of a water surface—often appeared.

"Well, hello there." A deep voice with a trace of a Southern accent spoke into her ear.

Suzette jumped.

"Sorry to scare you."

Golden curls glowed above the gray uniform that Suzette was getting used to seeing around. Her father was the Commandant of the school, the disciplinarian, the bad guy. *"Who would dare to hurt his daughter? Who would dare to date her, either,"* she thought glumly.

"No, that's okay. I was just looking at the water. I guess I didn't hear you walk up."

Skipper sniffed his pant leg, and the boy began scratching under the dog's bearded chin.

"I hear y'all just moved from Boston," he said, smiling. "How's Florida so far?

Suzette shaded her eyes and squinted at the dog. "It's hot."

"Yeah, I know. It's hot in Charleston, too. That's where I'm from."

"I'm sorry. Maybe you should go to boarding school in Boston."

He laughed.

21

"Good idea, but it's a little late for that. I'm a senior, so I graduate this year. Where are you going to school? Sanford High School? You could go to school here, but you wouldn't get much of an education—at least not in class. Guess that wouldn't fly with Pointdexter. I mean, our superintendent."

"You're right. There isn't the slightest possibility that Mr. Pointdexter would let me go to school here at the academy."

"That's a shame because we have one hell of a chemistry lab."

He grinned at her, and Suzette felt her face start flushing.

"Maybe we could hang out together?" he asked. "One night, before classes start?"

Hooray! A date! She would actually escape from her house and her parents for a few hours. She could flirt with a guy, a senior guy. Her mind raced. Maybe they could drive to the beach—wherever it was. Now that sounded interesting, until he started talking again.

"There's a great roof deck on top of the main school building. We could head up there, get high, and watch the stars."

She froze. "I… don't… smoke."

"Really?" he was still smiling, shaking his head, and seemed amused by her answer. "You're kidding, right?"

Suzette wanted to bolt from the sheer awkwardness of the situation. This guy was such an idiot. What kind of invitation was that? Is this what the local girls did? No ice cream, no drive, no dinner, no movie? Nothing but a stair climb to the roof and a joint? It was unbelievable…, and it scared her to death.

"Hey, Captain LeBlanc was looking for you on the Quarterdeck." Tim Russell joined them and stared at golden curls as he nodded toward the school building. His handsome features had hardened, and his shoulders were squared.

22

"Oh? Uh, later." With barely a glance at Suzette, the curly-haired guy walked away, and Tim's expression immediately softened.

"Be careful with that one," he said. "I'm not telling you what to do, but if you ever want to know more about a midshipman, well, just ask. I'm here."

He smiled.

"Thanks for the heads up," she said, picking up Skipper. "I guess I need a guide to this place. I've been gone so long, my mother probably thinks I fell in the lake. Gotta go."

As Suzette headed back to the apartment, she felt protected and just a little relieved. Someone here was looking out for her. Besides, she didn't even catch curly hair's name.

Suzette liked her father's assistant.

With that pale, porcelain skin and big blue eyes, Esther "Bunny" Phillips could be a knockout. Suzette was pretty sure she wore those ugly, black glasses to keep love-starved midshipmen at bay. Young, tall, and thin, she'd be the perfect crush. It was a good thing her husband taught Spanish and chorus at the school. Best of all, Bunny volunteered to be the cheerleaders' sponsor.

The Phillips didn't have kids. God, Suzette hoped Bunny didn't think of her as a kid. The woman probably was in awe of the number of bags the LeBlancs strolled in with after a mother-daughter shopping spree.

Bunny's red ponytail bobbed up and down as she waved enthusiastically from her desk.

"You two did some serious damage. Look at those shopping bags."

23

"Oh, nothing fancy," Mom said. "Just some essentials."

Any time Suzette and her mother ran into Bunny, she seemed delighted to see them. Suzette guessed it was because the secretary didn't have much opportunity for 'girl talk' during the day. After all, she worked for the Captain, and all the other secretaries in the building looked old enough to be her mother..., or grandmother even.

"We found every sale in Orlando," Mom gushed, delighted to share information with such an appreciative audience.

"Do you have the new pillows?" Mom asked Suzette as she rifled through the bags in her hands.

Suzette shook her head and looked through the ones she was holding.

Her mother snapped her fingers and tossed the car keys to her daughter. "I just remembered. They're in the trunk. Run and get them, please."

Suzette didn't mind. She jogged across the Quarterdeck to the front doors, dodging student boxes and suitcases. Today was move-in day for incoming freshmen, so there was more activity than usual. That's probably why she initially didn't notice the movement from a wooden bench beside the entrance. Of course, she wasn't wearing her glasses, either.

Members of the senior class had arrived a few days early to distribute information packets and assist the younger midshipmen as they settled into their rooms. Seniors were the guys in pressed uniforms, who looked calm and confident. New students were even easier to spot. Their expressions ranged from wide-eyed terror to sullen acceptance.

Somebody's father held the door open as Suzette hurried up the stairs. Her mother was still standing by Bunny Phillips's desk, so she made a beeline toward them. That's when she realized that three midshipmen had just leaped to their feet and stood at attention as she flew by.

Wait a minute. What just happened?

So, Suzette did what any curious person would do. She turned and walked past them, again.

This time, though, no one budged. The threesome remained glued to the bench.

She whirled and stopped dead in her tracks.

"Why didn't you stand up for me?"

"Statute of limitations. You've passed us too many times," one said with an arched eyebrow, obviously taking great pleasure in his statement.

Suzette felt her face flush and realized the joke was on her. Without her glasses, she couldn't even read the name tag on his uniform.

While it was customary for midshipmen to stand at attention for teachers, parents, senior staff, and women, she really didn't belong in any of those categories.

"*I never fit in anywhere,*" she thought.

A familiar Aretha Franklin song regarding respect began to play in her head.

Midshipman David Menaker helped a couple of new kids find their rooms before slipping out the French doors in the ballroom to the rear patio. He sat on a pitted-aluminum couch with plastic flowered cushions and blew smoke rings toward the sky. Life was good.

Last year, he'd had to sneak cigarettes or face demerits along with extra duty if he'd been caught, but he persuaded his father to sign the paperwork: Please sign and date this at the bottom to give permission for your child to smoke while a student at the

Sanford Naval Academy. Only those children who have parental permission and who remain in the designated smoking area on the rear patio will be allowed to do so. You are free to withdraw your permission for your child's participation at any time and for any reason without penalty. These decisions will have no effect on your future relationship with the school or your child's status or grades here.

Both his father and grandmother were thrilled that he was finishing high school. They would probably sign anything to keep him there. He'd dropped out after his sophomore year. Well, he didn't really drop out so much as he just quit going to classes. He slept in, smoked a little weed, and fell so far behind in academics, the school was going to make him repeat an entire year if he went back.

That was never going to happen.

Then his father approached him with a brochure for the Sanford Naval Academy. It didn't look too bad, and the place was even on a lake. As a kid, David loved watching parades and marching bands, so he decided to give the academy a shot. He would make the old man happy and get his high school diploma after all.

Now, as he sat in the smoking lounge and stared out at the lake, David smiled. His senior year already looked great. He was in the Ceremonial Guard Company, in the Key Club, and on *The Clipper* newspaper staff and had earned the nickname "The Menacer." Hell, he only joined the chorus because it would get him out of classes to perform at places like the Women's Club and the Chamber of Commerce, even a few churches. He'd even heard a rumor that the new commandant had a hot, blonde daughter.

Yeah, this was definitely going to be a good year.

26

CHAPTER 4
Passing Muster

English teacher Bruce Penn slid into a chair next to the Captain at a dinner table in the Mess Hall. It was Mr. Penn's turn as Staff Duty Officer (SDO), which meant for the next twenty-four hours, he was in charge. For the second time in two weeks, the family dined with the midshipmen, eating the best fried chicken Suzette and her mother had ever tasted. The Captain explained that Mr. Penn would spend the night upstairs in the designated SDO room and be available if kids wanted to talk or if the night watchman—known as the Rent-a-Cop to the midshipmen—spotted anything out of the ordinary.

Suzette didn't think Mr. Penn looked much older than his students, but tonight she noticed the instructor looked tired, though the sun hadn't even set.

"Cheers to the man in charge," said the Captain, hoisting his iced tea glass.

Mr. Penn sighed. "You know, every kid who is sent to boarding school has issues. I read a statistic that said seventy-five percent come from broken homes, and ninety-five percent of those are a result of divorce as opposed to the death of a spouse. The others come from homes where dad is busy with his medical practice, and mom is busy with her real estate business. These boys follow their teachers around like puppies because we pay attention to them."

Suzette listened intently.

The football coach, who was sitting with them, nodded. "I remember last year when one of my students was signing on to play football for the University of Georgia. His father hadn't come to a single high school game, but he made it for signing day. I think he was some kind of politician. Anyway, when I congratulated the kid on his football scholarship and having his dad there, he said, 'Coach, do you think he would miss a photo opportunity?'"

Mr. Penn reached for the salt, adding, "Men choose one of three roles as a parent: sperm donor, bank account, or a real father."

Suzette looked across the cafeteria and saw Bill Moore serving some of the younger boys seated at his table. Her father said that as a senior and the battalion commander, Moore was the highest-ranking student in the school. The kid was incredibly disciplined, and his uniform always looked impeccable. He actually enjoyed spending hours polishing his shoes. The Captain told her that Moore once gave himself demerits and served Extra Duty on the weekend because of his strong sense of honor.

"Moore's parents divorced when the boy was twelve, and the kid chose to escape family custody battles by enrolling in the academy," Mr. Penn said. "Rumor has it, the boy spotted an ad for the school in the back of a National Geographic magazine."

"He's roomed with Robbie Sherman ever since. Both boys are excellent students and have risen through the ranks," Mr. Penn added.

Mike McGrath stopped at the table to speak with the Captain. A junior according to academic records, "Big Mac" stood taller than most of the senior class and wider, too. According to the football coach, the guy boasted the perfect physique for an NFL lineman. Problem was, "Big Mac" didn't have a mean bone in his body. His size was merely one of the reasons the kid from Connecticut played Santa Claus at the annual Christmas party for orphaned children held at the academy each year.

Suzette's thoughts were interrupted by shrieks of laughter coming from another table where Tim Russell was seated, Tim, her hero, who warned her about that creepy golden-curls guy.

"Tim is quite the athlete," said Mr. Penn, following her gaze. "His family owns Florida citrus groves, and he dominates the track team as well as our state champion crew team. According to legend, he does pretty well with the cheerleading squad, too."

Suzette dug into a piece of fudge cake and studied the tall, tanned midshipman. She remembered meeting him when she and Mom took the dog for a walk. He seemed kind to the younger boys sitting around him, and they obviously worshipped Tim.

"If we had more kids like him, my job would be a lot easier," Mr. Penn said, as he cleared his tray.

Cotton ball clouds dotted a bright blue sky as Suzette walked to the gym for cheerleading practice. She arrived early and slid onto a bleacher to change into her saddle shoes. That's when she heard the sound of voices, even though the gym looked empty.

"Did you hear the screaming? God, it was so cool." He was laughing as he spoke.

"Purple water streaming out of your shower has a way of waking you right up," another said. "I heard Mr. Penn shouting over their screams to see what was wrong."

Suzette stopped tying her shoe and cocked her head to listen.

"Chemistry class used to be so boring: 'Potassium permanganate is an inorganic chemical compound," he droned, imitating the lectures. "It is also a strong oxidizing agent that is soluble in water, but be advised, when the two are mixed, it will produce intensely purple solutions."

"Hell, yes," the first boy snickered. "The secret is to dry the inside of shower heads really well before you sprinkle the chemicals inside and re-install them. I had plenty of time while the ninth graders were downstairs in Study Hall. I think new students need a proper welcome, especially the cocky ones. We're helping them make memories."

Suzette imagined the reaction of sleepy, young midshipmen as they stumbled into the shower and were doused with purple water. She scanned the gym but still couldn't see who was talking. She figured they must be in the locker room, where their voices would echo.

"Yeah. I heard in the early days, midshipmen were dumped in fields of mosquitoes in their underwear. Where did you get a key to the chemistry lab?"

"I collect 'em, every chance I get," the boy said. "The key to the barber shop comes in handy to sneak in and take my name off the haircut list. My real prize is the key to the maintenance shed, where the school vans are parked. You should come with me sometime to downtown Orlando and cruise Orange Blossom Trail. As long as we're back by dawn, it's cool."

Suzette would later learn it was David Menaker talking. No wonder they called him "The Menacer."

CHAPTER 5
The Compass

Fortunately for Suzette, half of the classrooms at Our Lady of Perpetual Guilt were air-conditioned. The library was, too, but students could go inside it only during their free periods. Most of the classrooms opened onto a sunny, tropical courtyard, lovely to look at but in reality, a broiler oven on the skin.

Sliding into a cool, metal desk for her first period English class usually made Suzette feel better. Her forty-five-minute bus ride in the early morning darkness left her uniform damp and stuck to her skin.

Due to a lucky break in the alphabetical seating chart, her desk was behind Mary Grace Laccona, a popular girl who seemed to know everyone in the school and was adored by all of them. Simply by listening, Suzette learned that she had two older brothers who were highly-revered football stars. One even played on the state championship team a few years earlier. Adding to the mystique, Mary Grace's father was a prominent attorney who represented well-known sports figures.

Suzette didn't care. She simply liked Mary Grace because the girl was smart and had an infectious laugh—two qualities she found invaluable in a friend. They talked about assignments, at first, before the English class started. Plus, Mary Grace was stellar at Spanish which was lucky for Suzette since the two girls spent every Friday afternoon in the library conjugating verbs. One day, Mary Grace waved her over to sit in the grass with a group of other girls during their shared lunch period. Suzette was grateful and a little relieved. Maybe she was beginning to crack the acceptance code.

One morning before class started, Suzette was surprised to find Mary Grace hunched over her desk with her head bowed.

"Hey, are you okay?"

"Fine. Got something in my eye."

Mary Grace sat up, pulled on her upper eyelid, and blinked rapidly.

"Even a speck of dust feels horrible under a contact lens."

Suzette straightened.

"You wear contacts?"

"Yeah. I have for a couple of years."

Suzette had always wanted contacts and hated wearing her glasses. She failed the school eye exam the first time in the fifth grade. A trip to the eye doctor revealed that she had 20/30 vision, which wasn't bad enough for corrective lenses. It was, however, bad enough to frustrate a tall girl who always was seated in the back of her elementary school classrooms and forced to squint at the board. The following year, her vision slipped to 20/80 and continued to deteriorate even further.

Suzette needed her glasses to see the board—the teacher, too—but as soon as class ended, she folded them into a case and dropped them into her purse.

"Boys don't make passes at girls who wear glasses," she had read somewhere.

Her mom spent hours helping Suzette pick out frames that didn't make her look like a hideous freak, but there really weren't a lot of styles to choose from. It was pink or blue frames for little kids. Eventually, she opted for gold, wire frames in hopes they might blend in with her hair and not be too noticeable.

Still, she hated wearing them.

The Captain acted like a complete jerk every time she asked about getting contacts.

"They're too expensive..., you'll lose one.... They're hard lenses and can break.... You're too young to be responsible for them...."

The list of excuses seemed endless and totally unfair to Suzette.

Here was Mary Grace, someone her own age, who had contact lenses. Her two older brothers did, too, and they played contact sports. If a lens was going to be lost or broken, it seemed a lot more likely to happen on a football field.

Suzette wrote down the name of the eye doctor and shared the information with her parents about it at the dinner table that night. Most of the time, they had dinner in their private quarters but at least one night each week—and anytime fried chicken was served—they ate with the boys.

The Captain shook his head, but her mother was insistent. "Paul, she'll be driving soon, and she needs to be able to see."

He waved a finger in the air.

"We can't afford to replace those things every time she breaks or loses one."

"Contacts don't break any more than eyeglasses break. I'm sure Suzette will be very careful."

He excused himself for a staff meeting and let the door slam behind him. Her mother picked up the sheet of notebook paper with the doctor's name on it and winked.

"I'll call tomorrow and schedule an appointment for you. We'll go after school, and we won't tell him."

Yeah, Mom.

Suzette suspected that not wearing her glasses didn't help her social life. She couldn't see far enough to recognize anyone, so she often appeared aloof, distant, and even snobbish. At least that's what she overheard some girls saying at her last school. Nobody realized that she just couldn't see them. Sometimes, she even felt like a freak because she was always squinting, but that was still better than wearing glasses.

Suzette LeBlanc never told anyone she was legally blind.

The tiny circles were tinted pale blue, primarily so that the wearer could spot them more easily in their white plastic case, but when the doctor popped one into Suzette's own blue eye, she noticed the effect was pretty spectacular.

Oddly enough, after a few tries, she had no qualms about inserting the lenses or removing them from her eyes. In fact, it was easier than she had imagined it would be. Alternately using the cleaning and wetting solutions was a breeze, and it didn't even hurt to blink with the lenses inserted.

As they walked to the car, Suzette noticed leaves on the trees and individual blades of grass that no longer looked like a blur of green color. Everything looked crisp and clear and completely fascinating. She stared at the world outside the doctor's office and began to realize how much she missed by refusing to wear her glasses.

"Wow, Mom, I can see! I can actually see!"

Her mother laughed. "No kidding? That ought to help a lot when you get your Learner's Permit and start driving. I'm looking forward to the day when I stop chauffeuring you around."

When they arrived home, Suzette hurried past her father, who was watching the nightly news from his leather recliner. She wanted to avoid another argument. He'd already changed out of his uniform and was holding a cocktail glass filled with brown liquid.

She put her contact lenses' case and bottles of solutions safely on a glass shelf in the bathroom before washing her face and wrapping up in a bathrobe. When Mom called her to dinner, she was surprised to see her father wasn't joining them at the table.

"Where's Dad?"

"He fell asleep in the chair, so I didn't wake him," Mom answered. "I'll make him a sandwich later if he's hungry."

Suzette felt relieved. She was excited about the afternoon's events and wanted to talk about it. Conversation always flowed easier without her father. Her mother noticed it, too.

They both knew he was different when he drank, though he never staggered or fell or missed a day at work. He never had car accidents, either and certainly was never hospitalized or jailed for drunkenness. Wasn't he entitled to relax with a few drinks in the evening before going to bed? At least that's what he always said.

Suzette cleared the dinner dishes as her mother answered a knock at their front door.

"I'm sorry; the Captain isn't available," her mother said to someone standing outside. "He isn't feeling well."

Suzette could see a midshipman crane his neck around her mother and look down the hall. She followed his gaze and could clearly see her father's hand reaching for his cocktail on the table next to the recliner. She turned back to see her mother stiffen slightly and begin to close the door.

"Is Dad sick?" Suzette asked, when her mom came back to the kitchen.

"What? Oh, no. He's taken some of that allergy medicine, and it really knocks him out. I don't want the boys to have to deal with him when he's like this."

"Allergy medicine?" Suzette thought. "Like the Scotch had nothing to do with it?"

She glanced uneasily down the hallway where the television still blared. She didn't want to deal with him, either.

CHAPTER 6
Wide Berth

The Captain always left his Navy hat decorated with the gold braid on the back seat of the Impala. Its black brim was covered in golden-oak-leaf embellishments nicknamed "scrambled eggs."

Suzette shoved it aside as she climbed into the car. "Why do they call them scrambled eggs? Those Navy guys were either bored or hungry when they decided on names for their hats."

"I really don't know," Mom said. "But your father is pretty proud of them. Only officers with a rank of commander or higher can wear those scrambled eggs."

Her mother opened the door on the passenger side as Tim Russell slid behind the steering wheel. Suzette hated to admit it, but she liked the fact that her mother wanted the midshipmen to feel important, trusted, and responsible. She always let them drive the family car whenever they went for a ride, ran errands, had doctor's appointments, and the like.

A half day of school gave them a free afternoon, and they ended up sitting at a picnic table outside an ice cream shop. Suzette's scoop started to melt as she held it, but she discovered that it tasted better when she let it sit for five minutes. She licked a ripple of fudge inside the vanilla ice cream, trying to keep it on her tongue instead of the roof of her mouth. Years of practice (and biology textbooks) proved it was the most effective way of delivering flavor to the 9,000 taste buds in her mouth. A waffle cone remained perfectly crunchy in her hand.

"Hey, thanks again for helping me with my uniform," Tim said to her mother. "Your husband is super fussy about frayed hems or holes. I don't know how to sew, and I don't want to buy new pants 'cause I'm never gonna wear 'em again once I graduate. In fact, I'll probably *burn* 'em."

"I'm glad I could help out," Mom said. "Come see me any time you have a problem like that."

Tim mentioned that several of the midshipmen were spending their free afternoon at Blue Spring State Park. He added that the spring was a favorite spot for swimmers, snorkelers, and certified scuba divers seeking to escape from the Florida heat because it had clear, seventy-three-degree water. Tim was kind of a human encyclopedia, always spewing trivia facts about Florida.

"Covering more than twenty-six hundred acres, including the largest spring on the St. Johns River, Blue Spring is a designated Manatee Refuge," he said. It was the manatees' winter home.

Of course, the guys had driven there in a car that was illegally stashed somewhere nearby. Her father had explained that midshipmen weren't allowed to have cars at school. It was stated clearly in the rules for admission, and most families were happy to comply. The cost of insurance for teenage male drivers was astronomical, her dad always said. The academy reduced its liability by not permitting students to have automobiles.

A grin spread slowly across Tim's face. "Hey, y'all want to go to Blue Spring?"

Minutes later, the Impala roared into the parking lot; a cloud of dust rose from the crushed oysters beneath the car tires. The Captain's hat perched on Tim's head while Mom, who agreed to the joke, ducked down beside him, and Suzette crouched in the backseat.

For a fleeting moment, time stopped. The boys immediately recognized the car since they watched for it often enough. Seeing only a man's profile wearing a familiar hat, the midshipmen erroneously believed their Captain had come to lock them in detention for a lifetime.

Peeking over the door, Suzette witnessed complete chaos— boys in swimsuits diving into the bushes, leaping into the water and scattering down paths into the underbrush. Tim burst out laughing and seemed utterly delighted by the success of his joke. As Suzette and her mother flung open the car doors, Tim began waving his arms and shouting, "It's okay. Y'all come out. It's just us."

One disheveled head peeked around a palmetto bush.

"Jeez, Russell, what are you trying to do? Give us a heart attack?"

Another boy appeared with scratches across his chest that resembled the faint outline of a palm frond.

"I'm going to kill you, man."

One more boy limped with a bleeding toe that he stubbed on the rocks along the edge of the spring. Several brushed dirt off of their skinned knees.

"We're sorry," Suzette apologized as she peeled off her stupid ankle socks and shoes to wade into the cool spring water. "Have you guys seen any manatees?"

"No, but there's a bunch of bass and turtles in here." One picked up his snorkel and mask from the ground, spitting into it to clear the fog.

"We're lucky it's still October 'cause the spring closes to all water-related activities like swimming, snorkeling, scuba diving, and boating from mid-November through March," said the boy with the bleeding toe. "They want it to be a safe, warm-water refuge for manatees during the winter."

"Here goes the human encyclopedia, again," Suzette thought, rolling her eyes.

"Last year, I watched 'The Forgotten Mermaids on a Jacques Cousteau show," Tim said. "Did you know it was filmed here? That documentary brought lots of attention to the manatee and the importance of Blue Spring. I think that's why the state of Florida bought this land and made it a park."

"I'm very glad they did," Mom said. "It's beautiful here."

Battalion commander Bill Moore sat on his bunk, shining his black uniform shoes. "Are you seeing your favorite cheerleader, Debbie, tonight?"

His roommate, Robbie Sherman nodded, closing his chemistry book. "Just for a little while. It's her dad's birthday."

It was a pretty uneventful day, Bill thought. The younger boys had all been out of bed and lined up outside their rooms when he'd walked the halls for morning inspection.

There even was a line for the barbershop when it opened at seven o'clock.

Bill knew that some midshipmen paid ten dollars to have their name removed from the Haircut Roster every two weeks. Some even stole the key to the barbershop, snuck in, and erased their names from the list. He hadn't caught them yet. He would, though. He was certain. Sometimes he hated that he was responsible for keeping things above board, but it was part of his job description.

As Battalion Commander and Executive Officer, Bill and Robbie ran the school's demerit system. They determined who served extra duty and who had liberty. They also conducted morning inspections, checking for cleanliness of uniforms, tidiness of bedrooms, and contraband—no food or drink was allowed in student quarters. (It kept the cockroach population down.)

Seniors were permitted to study in their rooms while underclassmen were herded to Study Hall in the Mess Hall. Tonight was quiet, and with only one more bed check before lights out, Robbie would never be missed. Rules could be bent, occasionally.

Always a perfectionist, Bill kept buffing until he heard the announcement from the Quarterdeck below. "Battalion Commander Bill Moore, please report to the Commandant's quarters immediately."

"I wonder what's up," he said, heading for the door. Robbie shrugged and grinned, adding a soft, "Good luck," as Bill headed for the stairwell.

Suzette answered the door.

"Your dad wanted to see me?" It was a question and a statement rolled into one.

"He's down the hall," she said with a wave of her hand. Bill could see spiral notebooks scattered all over the beds in her room, and she promptly headed back to her assignments.

"Ahhhh, Mr. Moore," the Captain purred from his recliner. "Where is Mr. Sherman this evening?"

Bill paused but answered truthfully. "He was in our room when I left, sir."

"I'd like to see him."

"Yes sir," Bill replied and walked out of the apartment to head back into the school. How could the captain possibly know about Robbie's date? He was pretty sure Suzette would never say anything to her father, since she and Debbie were good friends. Was the man psychic?

By the time Bill reached the academy's front doors, he saw Debbie's yellow station wagon pull away from the curb.

That's when he started running.

He could see the stoplight ahead turn red and thought he could make it. Just as he got close, the light turned green, and the station wagon eased forward.

"Shit." He was gasping for air by the time he reached the next intersection and banged on the car window.

"What in the world is wrong?" asked Debbie, as she rolled it down. Bill struggled for breath.

"LeBlanc... wants... Robbie," he heaved, flinging the rear door open and hurling himself into the back seat.

The station wagon made it back to the academy in seconds, and both midshipmen scurried into the building, trying to draw as little attention to themselves as possible. Bill knocked on the Captain's door a second time, and Suzette yanked it open, raising an eyebrow as she motioned for the pair to continue down the hallway toward her father's chair.

"You know, I've got homework to finish, so why don't I just leave the door unlocked so you can come and go whenever you want?"

"Sorry." Bill raised both hands in defeat as he walked by her.

"Ahhhh, Mr. Sherman. I'm glad to have you setting a fine example for the troops." The Captain studied him for several minutes after inviting both boys to sit down. He turned abruptly to Bill.

"I don't know how in the hell you did it, son, but you're good."

The learning curve on midshipmen's antics for the new commandant had been steep, but he was catching on.

CHAPTER 7
Keelhauling

After practice, the cheerleaders' nightly ritual was to head to the cooler in the LeBlanc's kitchen for a cup of ice water. Suzette couldn't taste any difference, but Mom swore that Florida tap water tasted like sulphur, so she had the enormous glass bottles of spring water delivered every month.

They barely sat down at the table when a bell signaling study hall break started ringing, and Janice was on her feet.

"Thanks, Mrs. LeBlanc, but I've got some homework to finish, so we've got to go."

Debbie and Suzette followed her to the front door, which opened to a grassy lawn area beside the school. Since the Mess Hall closed after serving dinner every evening, many midshipmen headed to vending machines located in a hospital across the street for snacks.

A short walk in the night air and bags of M&Ms or potato chips definitely cleared the head.

The girls were standing under a street light beside the school when a few midshipmen stopped to talk. Robbie arrived and squeezed Debbie's hand about the same time the football coach walked up to join the group. In the confusion, Suzette didn't notice Janice slip away until the rest of the crowd started to thin out.

Midshipmen were headed back to their rooms for evening bed check when Suzette spotted the lovers emerging from the shadows behind a classroom building. Their arms were around each other's waists, and Janice was leaning into him, which struck Suzette as a little odd. She noticed the guy had never been physically demonstrative with Janice in front of other people. Suzette guessed it was because he enjoyed flirting with any girl in the vicinity.

"Let's go guys. Back to the books," the coach said, grinning. The midshipmen trailed him into the building as Suzette turned to the girls.

"I just made love," Janice sighed.

"Where?" Suzette was appalled.

"In the grass behind the classrooms."

It actually sounded wet and buggy to Suzette, rather than romantic.

"I don't even care if I'm pregnant," she gushed. "He's so wonderful, and I love him. I just have to get rid of this rash before I go home."

"Rash?"

"Every time we make love, I break out in a rash across my chest. I just don't want my mom to see it."

Suzette winced a little. She had never heard of sex causing a rash on your chest, maybe other places, but that was a venereal disease, wasn't it? She'd never had a friend who was having sex like Janice, so she really didn't know how to respond.

"Um, maybe you should just jump in the shower when you get home," Suzette suggested.

"Yeah, that might work. If my mom walks into my room and sees my chest, she'll think I rubbed too hard with the towel."

Suzette's head spun with everything she'd just been told, but it felt like an alien world that she couldn't relate to at all. "Not all education occurs in a classroom setting," she thought.

CHAPTER 8
Above Board

School was going pretty well, and the cheerleading season was finishing up. Suzette spent most of her weekdays at school, her afternoons at cheerleading practice, and her weekends hanging out with the girls from the squad.

The black "River Maybelline" ran down Janice's face, from her perfectly curled eyelashes to her chin. Janice wore a ton of makeup and some outfits that seemed rather tight to Suzette.

"Sh-she called me a slut...; my own mother called me a slut."

Suzette could feel her mouth opening to say something comforting, but the words running through her brain refused to form a sentence.

"I'm pregnant."

So that was the problem. Suzette knew little about Janice's romantic life since she stopped dating midshipmen. Well, now that she thought about it, she did hear the older girls once ask her who the mystery man was.

"I'm so sorry."

Actually, Suzette didn't know exactly what she felt sorry about: The pregnancy or the exploding relationship between Janice and her mother? Maybe the wasted tube of mascara?

"What are you going to do?"

"Keep my baby, of course."

Suzette was shocked. The few times she had been asked to babysit, she hated it. There were jars of slimy food, hot bottles and diapers—God, she hated changing dirty diapers. Janice was only three years older. How could she possibly consider having a baby? It's so *permanent*. She would never have a life.

"My mom actually asked me how many times we had sex," Janice blew her nose. "She wanted a numerical count. She even wants to know where. I'm not telling the bitch anything, of course. She's never even met my boyfriend. She probably thinks he's one of the midshipmen at the academy. God, my crazy brother would kill him if he found out."

Suzette had seen Janice's brother. Six feet tall and six feet wide, Joe played on the Sanford High School football team. He seemed to have a single, bushy eyebrow growing straight across his forehead.

"Ummm, is your boyfriend happy about you having the baby?"

"I haven't told him, yet," Janice sniffed. "He just took a job in Jacksonville, and I was waiting 'til we could see each other, you know, face to face."

A job? Uh-oh, the situation is sounding worse.

"He's twenty-three and training at the shipyard. He's going to make a lot of money. Plus, we're so in love. He's amazing."

Janice smiled, and Suzette wasn't sure whether it was intended to reassure herself or Suzette. However, she did know that the laws in this state and a lot of others, say a twenty-three-year-old man can't date a seventeen-year-old girl. She had heard the midshipmen joking about it. Well, he can, but authorities technically call it *rape*.

"I swear I won't tell anyone about your boyfriend, Janice."

"Thanks, Suzette," Janice wiped her nose. "You're the only one who knows."

"What about your senior year?"

Suzette knew it sounded like a ridiculously dumb question, but at the moment, she couldn't seem to think of a better one.

46

"I'll probably just get my GED. High school is sooooo boring. I'll have to drop out of cheerleading because the uniform won't fit me in a couple of months. You can step into my spot, right? You won't be an alternate on the squad anymore."

Always looking for the bright spot... that Janice.

Suzette was thrilled when she mastered a series of jumps that the cheerleading squad demanded. Still no split, but to be honest, she wasn't trying very hard. Her thigh muscles twitched dangerously every time she attempted it, and she assumed it was her body's version of a Morse Code, spelling D-A-N-G-E-R. She could leap airborne like a stag, and that was an impressive enough feat for her.

Practice ended, and the girls left the gym, hauling their shoes and pom-poms. The soles of their saddle shoes were white, so the experienced cheerleaders instructed Suzette to take them off before walking across asphalt streets and concrete sidewalks. Otherwise, she would be required to scrub them clean or paint them white.

The night air was cool, and nobody seemed to be in much of a hurry to go home.

"Want to come in for a minute, Janice? You left your brush and stuff in my bedroom Friday night," Suzette asked.

The older girl would stop by the apartment before every game. After five minutes spent checking her hair and makeup in front of a mirror, Janice headed for the quarterdeck to flirt with guys. Suzette realized that living in the same building as the midshipmen added to her popularity with girls on the squad and provided a convenient excuse for them to visit.

Debbie walked along, too, since she needed a ride home.

47

"Hi, Mrs. LeBlanc."

"Hi, girls. You look exhausted. Can I get you something cool to drink?"

Suzette knew that her mother was wary of the girls. She prayed the woman would never hear about Janice's situation. God knows Suzette would never tell her. She learned from her older sister how to withhold information: "When Mom asks you to confirm a rumor that you know is true, it's best to start with 'I understand that....' It isn't exactly a lie because you totally understand, but it also distances you from the rumor and makes you more of an observer than a participant in the crime."

After the girls left, Suzette's mother asked her directly about Janice's baby. Suzette was shocked. Did the woman have radar? Still, her mother probably felt relieved since Suzette wouldn't see much of Janice any more. Unmarried and pregnant teens were hidden, mysteriously disappearing from their schools and homes until after they delivered their babies. Suzette had known a girl in her school up north who was pregnant, and Suzette remembered the secrecy, as well as the stigma, surrounding it. Because of the shame of having a child out of wedlock, many girls gave up their child for adoption. Suzette doubted that Janice would, but why should it matter?

Janice was only one out of ten girls on the squad, yet Mom acted like sex was a chapter in the cheerleading handbook. The rest of the girls were getting ready for college, and they weren't pregnant. Why did her mother make such a big deal out of everything?

CHAPTER 9
Tacking

Suzette never understood why she needed to read "Dante's Inferno." She lived in it. The bus ride from her high school in Orlando to her home in Sanford lasted forty-five minutes in the heat. Even with the bus windows open and a slight breeze lifting pages of a notebook on the seat beside her, it was scorching.

At least she had an entire seat to herself. There were so few kids from Sanford, everyone had claimed their own seat on the first day of school. Suzette looked at the boy across the aisle who slunk down in his seat every afternoon with headphones plugged into a radio and his eyes closed. Nearby, a girl with glasses and curly hair always piled books on the seat beside her and stared out the window for the duration of the trip.

Suzette knew that many of these kids were brothers and sisters. They all looked alike.

There were so many blond heads on this bus, it could be headed for Hitler's youth camp.

Just like the naval academy, this was another local tribe where everyone either knew each other—or was related—and Suzette did not belong.

Florida's heat caused her oil glands to work overtime, especially the ones in her hair and on her face. The back of her white cotton blouse stuck to her skin like Saran wrap. She was sure the ankle socks contributed to her misery. They made everyone hotter in the worst possible way.

Most days, she got home around four o'clock, and after poaching for an hour on a vinyl bus seat, she had just enough energy to peel off her uniform and collapse on the bed. Heat exhaustion is a terrible thing—she knew that she could never choose a career as a landscaper or any other outdoor job.

Eventually, she wandered into the kitchen looking for ice water, iced tea, or really anything ice cold to drink. That's when she noticed a midshipman standing in the flower bed outside the dining room windows. He was cleaning them, actually, with ammonia and a rag. He waved and grinned. Suzette was pretty sure Mom would have him sitting at their dinner table later that night like she always did when she asked midshipmen to help with a household chore.

Suzette couldn't figure out how her mother did it, really. The woman coerced midshipmen to move furniture, carry in groceries, and now, wash windows. Their efforts succeeded in making Suzette look bad since she never volunteered, but she suspected they probably didn't help their own mothers when they were at home either.

"Does anyone ever feel appreciated by the people they are related to?" she thought.

After a shower, Suzette changed into a loose T-shirt and baggy shorts and walked back to the kitchen. She found "Big Mac," the midshipman who had been cleaning the windows, sitting at the dining room table with Skipper in his lap.

"Hey there; how was your day?" he asked.

His face was as red as hers had been thirty minutes earlier, and he sipped a Coke over ice.

"Fine," Suzette answered. "I've got a report due for my 'Comparative Religions' class, and I'm just not into it. You know?"

"I feel for you. I really do," he said. "I hated the Catholic school that I went to in Connecticut..., all those nuns."

"Well, I've only got a couple of teachers who are nuns," Suzette said. "The rest are all lay people."

"Good for you." He nodded. "That probably works out a lot better. I've always wondered how nuns could relate to kids. I mean, they never had any of their own."

Mom carried in a plate of chocolate chip cookies, still warm from the oven.

"I was stuck in a class of twenty-six kids taught by a Dominican nun who had no idea how to help me with my reading disability," he continued. "She just skipped over me and called on someone else. At the end of the year, she held me back, and I had to repeat the grade."

He chewed on a cookie and glanced at a clock on the wall.

"Gosh, it's four thirty? Would you excuse me for a minute? I need to go to the bookkeeper's office and pick up my cash before he closes for the day."

Every Thursday and Friday afternoon, the bookkeeper distributed a small allowance to each midshipman. It wasn't much, but it allowed them to go to a movie, play pool, or grab a bite to eat over the weekend.

Suzette had heard boys talking about the Ship's Store, a converted classroom that sold pencils, stationery, candy bars like Snickers and Milky Ways, bags of potato chips, pretzels, and T-shirts.

"My shoe felt empty this morning."

Seeing Suzette's puzzled expression, he elaborated.

"Since some people walk into our rooms upstairs and steal, I hide my cash under the cushion in my shoe. If you're not creative in hiding your money, you'll be very poor."

"Come back because I have a roast for dinner, and I need your help eating it," Mom called after him.

Her mother genuinely cared about these guys; she really did, and Suzette guessed that midshipmen recognized that affection and responded to it. Of course, escaping from the Mess Deck to a home-cooked dinner probably didn't hurt either.

After searching the house for her algebra book, Suzette found it on the floor beside the living room couch. As she bent to retrieve it, she could hear her parents talking in their bedroom.

"I don't know why we're constantly feeding these boys at our dinner table," the Captain said. "Their parents pay for room and board here."

"I want to get to know them," her mother replied. "If they feel like part of the family, they'll be less likely to take advantage of our daughter."

The sailing team captain felt the sweat trickling down his forehead. At least that's how he explained it to Suzette the next day.

"We needed twenty cans across the bottom to form the base."

They carried a bag of empty beer cans from its hiding place in the boat house. One boy even raided a Boy Scout recycling bin for extra cans. They'd hidden some in their rooms, of course, but didn't want to risk lifelong detention by stashing upstairs the quantity they needed.

"Such a sweet project."

After practicing in the boat house, the boys devised an efficient plan: two knelt on the floor to stack while two quietly passed cans from the bags. Silence was imperative since any loud crashes would surely wake the Captain's daughter.

"Her bedroom is just inside the front door," one cautioned, as they crept down the corridor. "Absolutely no talking, or we'll get killed."

The group worked quickly and methodically until a pyramid of beer cans rose more than five feet from the floor and completely blocked the doorway. As a final touch, one midshipman grabbed the camera that hung from a leather strap around his neck and snapped a few pictures for posterity, maybe even the school yearbook.

It looked amazing, an aluminum tower glinting in the corridor security lights. The group headed up the nearest stairwell, careful to avoid the rent-a-cop on his rounds.

Miraculously, Suzette never heard a thing...that is, until her father pulled open the front door on his way to watch the battalion's morning formation.

"Good luck at school today."

His head was turned toward his daughter's bedroom, and he wasn't looking in front of him as he walked. Suzette started to say thanks, but her mouth simply hung open as she watched a shower of red, white, and blue beer cans spill inside the apartment, burying her father's feet.

The Captain's hand still gripped the door knob.

"God damn it." His face flushed an angry shade of red, and Suzette watched the muscles in his jaw tighten.

One of his freshly-polished, black shoes kicked beer cans aside. Then he was gone.

"MOM!" Suzette yelled down the hallway as Skipper started to growl.

The stench of stale beer reached her nostrils, and she noticed one can crunched between the door and the frame, preventing it from closing. She heard her mother gasp at the sight and then she started to giggle.

"I'll get a trash bag to clean this up. When it comes to pranks, those boys are very creative; aren't they?"

It was still dark when her mother drove her to the local Catholic Church parking lot to get on a bus in the morning. Unfortunately, the lack of padding on steel, bench bus seats made it impossible to sleep despite the darkness.

At the end of the day, when she finally flung open the door to the apartment at the Academy, Suzette's hair and skin felt sweaty and greasy. It was definitely not her best look or her best mood.

Totally devoid of energy, she lugged her textbooks into the living room and was dismayed to see midshipman Dougie stretched out on the couch under a blanket.

"What's he doing here?"

"Shhhhh—he's got a terrible throat infection and can barely breathe. We're waiting for test results to see if it's strep, so I made up the couch for him to stay here."

"Don't they have a school nurse for this kind of stuff?"

Suzette was annoyed. She didn't want to share her house or her mother with a ninth-grade Asian boy who was small for his age and could pass for a ten-year-old.

"I'm not sending him upstairs to his room alone. Suppose his throat closes up? That young man has a 102-degree fever, and he may need antibiotics to clear this infection up. I took him to the emergency room this morning."

Dougie opened dark black eyes and waved weakly as Suzette turned to her mother and rolled her own.

"He won't bother you. He can barely breathe. All he does is sleep, but I'm going to try to get him to eat some soup."

"He's spending the night, too?"

"Honestly, Suzette, where is your Christian charity?" her mother asked. "Don't be so grumpy."

A few times, Suzette tried to invite girls from her school home, but their reaction was always the same. "You live in Sanford?" They looked incredulous and never came.

She was grateful to be included in parties at someone else's house, but her situation was different. For starters, it wasn't a regular house. It was more like a dormitory with boys in uniforms coming and going to see her father.

In other words, it was extremely awkward.

Worst of all, Sanford was too far away from Orlando. Suzette guessed that most parents of her Catholic-school classmates refused to drive an hour to drop off or pick up their daughters. That's why Suzette was delighted to be invited to Mary Grace's house one Friday afternoon to help with an annual family ritual: the baking of a Yule Log cake.

"My mom will pick me up around six," Suzette said as they climbed into Mary Grace's brother's car.

"That should be enough time. Noona, my grandmother, usually does this with me. She's a fabulous cook and makes the most amazing Italian dishes. She hasn't been feeling well, so I thought I'd surprise her and make it myself."

The kitchen wasn't large, but there was enough room for both girls to work along the counter.

"The eggs are still cold, but we've got to separate them. Put the whites in one bowl and the yolks in another. They've got to get to room temperature before we use them. That usually takes about thirty minutes."

Suzette watched as Mary Grace buttered a long baking pan. Then she lined the pan with parchment paper, buttered, and floured it, too.

"You don't go to many of our football games or other stuff on the weekends, do you?" Mary Grace asked, beating egg yolks and sugar with an electric mixture.

"Well, I cheer for the naval academy and lots of times, their games are on the same night as ours. Plus, it's a really long drive from Sanford, so nobody wants to give me a ride home."

"Good point." Mary Grace laughed as she scraped down the sides of the bowl and added melted chocolate. "So how is it living at a boys' school? Do you like it? I mean, it sounds kind of weird."

"Sometimes it's fun," Suzette admitted. "There's always stuff going on, and guys are always around to see my father, but it's hard to have guy friends. Well, maybe hard isn't the right word. It's different. I can't talk to them the same way I talk to a girlfriend, you know?"

Mary Grace stuck her finger in the bowl to taste the batter and nodded for Suzette to do the same. Swirling the sweet dark sludge in her mouth, Suzette thought it tasted like heaven.

"I totally get it," Mary Grace said, licking her lips. "I've got two brothers who are incapable of discussing anything other than sports and food. Conversation is not their strong suit."

Mary Grace's father walked through the kitchen door, dropped his briefcase, and enveloped his daughter in a big bear hug.

"Daddy, this is my friend, Suzette. You've heard me talk about her before. She's the one who moved here from Boston."

He planted a kiss on his daughter's forehead and grinned at both girls. He was short, plump, and wore glasses, but his smile was infectious. When he looked at his daughter, he practically glowed. It was obvious that he adored her.

"Well, it's nice to meet you, Suzette. I hope we'll see a lot more of you around here."

"Thank you, sir. I hope so, too."

Suzette couldn't remember if her own father had ever greeted her so warmly. She picked up a timer from the kitchen counter and twisted it for fifteen minutes as Mary Grace instructed. Unfortunately, she twisted it in the wrong direction and wound up holding half of a broken timer in each hand.

"Cook much?" Mary Grace asked.

"I guess not enough. I'm sorry. When I do, I never use a timer. I normally just watch the clock."

Suzette plunged into the sink of dirty bowls and pans with a sponge. At least she knew how to clean up.

They chatted as they worked, and Suzette remembered how nice it was to have another girl to confide in rather than compete with. There were distinct advantages to having a friend who seemed genuinely interested in her, unlike the academy cheerleaders who seemed more interested in where she lived.

Mary Grace's mother came in with her coffee cup. She politely asked if Suzette had any brothers or sisters and then admired the Yule Log, a deliciously moist, chocolate sponge cake filled with chocolate whipped cream.

"You know, girls, the number of family members we get is limited, but we can expand our network of friends as long as we live." She paused, and Suzette wondered how the woman she had just met seemed to recognize her own isolation.

"Most of us will never save a life by running into a burning building, but science now tells us that we might just extend someone's life simply by being a part of it."

Somewhere in the house they heard a doorbell ring, and Mary Grace's brother called out, "Suzette, your mom is here."

"This was a lot of fun. Thanks so much for inviting me."

"I'm glad you could come. I'll let you know when Noona is making her homemade pasta. You'll love it! Just don't touch her timer."

CHAPTER 10
Man the Rails

Occasionally, Suzette could hear the midshipmen's voices drifting down from their rooms upstairs. Standing at the pedestal sink, she noticed a three-foot, louvered grate on the wall above the bathtub, which acted like a megaphone. The ancient porcelain tiled walls and tub formed a perfect echo chamber for the guys' laughter and music.

She hated to admit it, but sometimes, she actually felt a bit jealous that they had roommates and friends up there. She had…a dog and two parents, who did not provide a rollicking good time at night.

She had gotten used to hearing the noises, so she didn't pay much attention to the first grunt. An unmistakable thud, however, definitely got her attention, and Skipper began to growl.

Suzette flipped on the overhead light in her bathroom and saw nothing. No shampoo bottles were overturned, and no hairbrush appeared on the floor. Looking up, she noticed something twinkling behind the grate, something metallic, and it sounded like someone breathing very hard.

Her heart started pounding, but instead of feeling frightened, she found herself angrier than anything else.

"Hey. Who's up there?"

"I-I-I'm sorry, ma'am."

Her brain spun. Suzette knew that voice from somewhere.

"Dougie, is that you?"

It was the sick little Asian kid who had crashed on their couch. Suzette had seen him in the Captain's office many times for discipline problems and heard her father lamenting his behavior.

"Y-Y-Yes. I think I'm stuck."

"What are you doing in the ductwork?"

She heard a hissing sound from somewhere behind him.

"I, uh, well…, I lost something."

Suzette figured she would need a tall stepladder to get to the grate and probably a screwdriver, too. That's when an awful, devious thought occurred to her.

"Dougie, do you have a camera up there?"

Of course—send the smallest kid down the ductwork to take pictures of the Captain's daughter in the shower—if they could time it right.

Suzette wanted to kill someone; she just wasn't sure, who.

"Pull me out!" Dougie was shouting to someone behind him now.

"I can't—unless I get a ladder and my father to help me."

"No, please, wait."

Dougie was wailing now, and Suzette really didn't blame him. Metal ductwork couldn't be very comfortable. In fact, he was probably feeling a bit claustrophobic. It served him right.

"Don't call your father. I…ouch."

Suzette heard more thuds. She figured that kid would have nightmares for years.

"I'm sorry. I'm really sorry." Then his voice shifted, as if he was turning away from Suzette, and it rose almost to a squeak.

"Get me outta here."

The giggle in her throat—the kind that usually starts in a church pew and erupts into uncontrollable fits of laughter—began. She turned off the bathroom light and closed the door to her bedroom.

"You don't have to be crazy to live here, but it helps," she thought.

A few days later, Suzette stopped by Bunny Phillips' desk to pick up a cheerleading schedule when she spotted Dougie sitting in her father's office. The door was open, so she could hear their conversation clearly.

"A big part of who you become in life has to do with who you choose to surround yourself with," the Captain said. "It's better to be alone than in bad company. Distancing yourself from these people is never easy, son. To a certain degree, luck controls who walks into your life, but you decide who you spend the majority of your time with."

Suzette wondered what Dougie had done now? She couldn't wait around to find out. Cheerleading practice started in half an hour, and she needed to eat something first.

She knew that the Captain donned his white gloves and picked one wing of the school to inspect every Wednesday. She heard him talking about it to her mother. If a midshipman's room passed inspection, the boy was allowed to leave campus on liberty for a few hours later in the afternoon.

Tim told Suzette that her father walked slowly and methodically, inspecting beds, drawers, and closets as the battalion commander trailed behind him, taking copious notes.

While they were analyzing rooms along the opposite wing, someone punched a can opener into the bottom of a shaving cream canister and lobbed it like a hand grenade into Dougie's freshly-made bed. White foam arched along the wall and continued to spew as it rolled along the floor.

"Oh noooooooooooo...." the wailing began when Dougie saw the mess.

"Cleanliness is next to Godliness," a deep voice intoned, as it faded down the hallway. "Dougie should feel very holy by dinner."

The kid shifted his weight from one foot to the other.

"So, can you uh, help me out?"

The Menacer sighed. He told Suzette that he never meant to start a business. He altered one driver's license for a seventeen-year-old buddy so he'd have someone to drink with—or send on a beer run—since eighteen was the legal drinking age.

He'd accidentally discovered that having a military haircut and uniform actually had some benefits: Bouncers who guarded the doors of bars and clubs generally let servicemen in without checking their IDs too closely. Convenience store clerks also were more accommodating.

After The Menacer made a couple of fake licenses for midshipmen at the academy, word got out. Suddenly, he had a lucrative business—for twenty bucks, a new license could be yours.

He looked at the kid standing in his doorway. Tall with broad shoulders, he might pass for older.

"Okay, first you need a picture of yourself. Have someone take it against a blank background in really bright lighting, and keep the frame focused around your face. You shouldn't be able to see your shoulders in it."

"Can I use my passport photo?"

"Let's see it."

The kid pulled an envelope from his shirt pocket. The picture looked pretty good.

"I need your full name, but don't use any abbreviations."

"Unless you want to use an abbreviation like "John Smith, Jr." or "Thomas Jones, III.""

He eyed the boy.

"We've got to put in a realistic birth date. You can't have a license that says you were born in 1951 when you look twelve. It has to be believable."

"Don't forget to match the hair and eye color to your photo," The Menacer added. "These are the abbreviations."

He slid a sheet of paper across his desk. BRO—Brown, SDY—Sandy, BLK—Black, BLN—Blonde, RED—Red.

The true secret of The Menacer's success was the raised seal he'd stolen from his father, an electrical engineer who used it to certify blueprints—also, the iron he requested from his grandmother, who was impressed that he cared so much about his uniform appearance. It was a little tricky to use because if the iron got too hot, it melted the laminate plastic, yet, it had to be hot enough to bond the laminate to the fake ID.

The Menacer also had to be sure the iron didn't have any water loaded into it because that could damage the ink. He learned the hard way that steam could warp an ID card. After a bit of trial and error, he figured out how to cover the card with a towel, t-shirt, or even a paper bag. That kept the plastic from melting and sticking to the iron.

"I'll have it ready in a day or so. I have to wait until it's cooled off to trim the plastic about a quarter inch from the edge of the paper with an X-Acto knife. It's an art, really."

The kid grinned and handed over a twenty-dollar bill.

CHAPTER 11
Ballast

Suzette sat at the dining room table editing Tim's English paper for him. It wasn't very long, and she was happy to do it. Sometimes Suzette asked her mother to read her own term papers before turning them in, but midshipmen didn't exactly have their mothers handy.

Requests for help with algebra or geometry? Forget it.

Fortunately, spelling and grammar were easy for Suzette, so she didn't mind.

Another boy peeked around the corner and joined the group as Mom fetched him a Coke. She was wearing a navy-blue football jersey, emblazoned with "#1 MOM" across the back—a recent gift from the academy Key Club.

The Captain just finished a meeting with his senior staff in the living room, and one by one, the midshipmen wandered in and sat down at the table or on the floor next to Skipper.

"Hello, gentlemen," Mom said.

Evidently, no one was in much of a hurry to return to their rooms upstairs.

Suzette thought her mother could run a soda fountain. She watched the woman cut into a pan of brownies and breathe in the luscious, chocolaty aroma. Mom should have had more children—she loves this.

Suzette finished the paper and excused herself to run to the bathroom. When she returned, Mom and her adopted sons were laughing loudly in the dining room, and Suzette tripped over Tim who sat cross-legged on the floor as he rubbed Skipper's belly. The topic of discussion was weekend plans.

"My girlfriend and I are heading to the beach to celebrate our anniversary," he announced.

"Wow."

Suzette tried to sound sarcastic, like big deal—a beach. Florida is covered in them. Doesn't sound like much of an anniversary treat.

"We've got a room overlooking the water," Tim added, clearly annoyed at her lack of appreciation for his plans. "The shower is big enough for two, so we can wash each other's hair."

He was gloating, then, sensing her shock. Suzette struggled to keep her expression neutral, like she discussed this sort of thing every day… at lunch…, in the cafeteria of her parochial high school…, with Sister Mary Margaret listening.

Yeah, right.

In truth, it boggled Suzette's mind. She was still trying to figure out how to use a tampon, and Tim was taking showers with his girlfriend, presumably, right after they roll out of bed.

The thought startled her, and she felt like she must be developmentally delayed somehow. She knew that her figure looked okay, a little too thin, maybe, but a bit of padding in her bra made her look less like Popeye's girlfriend, Olive Oyl.

It's not that Suzette wanted to have sex with anyone. She didn't. There were practical reasons, of course, like protecting herself from sexually transmitted diseases or an unplanned pregnancy, but it was much more than that. She wanted to protect herself, emotionally. Suzette's mother and, of course, everyone else at Catholic school, preached the virtues of no sex before marriage.

She also had no idea how people found the time and the privacy to have sex…, normal people, that is, who have parents with the irritating tendency to be at home most of the time.

She didn't know any other couples who had the freedom—and the financial means—to simply book a hotel room.

Later that night, Suzette found Mom painting a set of louvered doors white.

They'd arrived from the hardware store as plain, unfinished wood, but that made them look like they belonged in some Western saloon rather than an apartment in the naval academy.

Still, her mother wanted something to block the view.

Many evenings, midshipmen would arrive at the door, asking to see the Commandant. When her mother said he wasn't available, the boys simply looked past her and saw the Captain sprawled in his chair. Mom just wanted to be sure they didn't see him drunk.

He was physically there, but mentally? Elvis had left the building.

By the seventh grade, Suzette learned to dread the sound of ice cubes hitting his glass because the gurgle of Scotch pouring from a bottle quickly followed.

Her father was pleasant until the family finished dinner. Then, settled in a recliner as he watched the nightly news, his mood grew darker and more argumentative. There were big fights with Mom, and one night when Big Mac came in to talk, the Captain stumbled and nearly fell. The midshipman caught her father by the elbow and helped him back to his chair. That's when Suzette noticed Big Mac stared intently at her. He seemed to be telegraphing, "I've got this. It's okay. I can keep a secret."

Despite the Captain's promises to change when they moved to Florida, the predictable pattern had returned. Ice cubes clinked, and the glass was refreshed until, by nine o'clock, he was snoring in an upright position, mouth agape, and any ability to deal with midshipman issues was long gone.

So, her mother installed the louvered doors in the hallway.

The woman had spent most of her life covering up for him and making excuses. Suzette learned by example that she shouldn't let the rest of the world know what was going on. Who would believe her, anyway?

*The doors protect the captain as much as the midshipmen. They just don't protect m*e, she thought.

CHAPTER 12
Flotsom

Fortunately, the white, roll-up-sleeve blouses Suzette wore to Our Lady of Perpetual Guilt also did double-duty under her cheerleading vest. That saved a bit of time.

It was after six o'clock, and she was buttoning the last button when the doorbell rang. She grabbed the navy-and-gold pleated uniform skirt lying on her bed and zipped it as she flung open the front door.

"Hey, there." Debbie's pom-poms rustled as she walked past Suzette into her bedroom. She leaned into the mirror and checked her makeup.

"The squad is meeting at the stadium at six-thirty."

Suzette was lacing on a saddle shoe when Debbie pivoted and headed back to the front door.

"I want to say hi to Robbie before we go."

Of course, she did. It was okay though since Suzette needed to cover up a rather obstinate pimple on her chin and pop her contacts in. She discovered it was easier to cheer when she could see what was happening on the field, and she refused to wear her glasses. Suzette had never seen a cheerleader with glasses...; it was probably a national rule or something.

When Debbie burst back through the door and announced they had five minutes to get to the field or be fined, Suzette shouted to her mother.

"I'm riding with the girls."

They sprinted down the sideline just as the squad started warm-ups. Suzette wasn't sure whether it was the lights or the night sky or the energy from the stands, but there was something exciting about a football stadium. Even when you know your team can't possibly win—and the best outcome simply may be no trips to the emergency room—it was still exciting.

She inhaled the scent of freshly-mowed grass and reached down to pick up her pom-poms when the head cheerleader tapped her on the shoulder.

"Ummm, Suzette, you're not wearing uniform pants."

She discreetly peeked and saw flowered panties. Crap. Debbie's last-minute arrival had distracted her, and she forgot to grab the navy-blue cover-up pants from her top drawer. There was no time to go home and retrieve them.

The head cheerleader wasn't happy.

"I guess you can help us lead cheers sitting in the stands."

Suzette did but noticed that wooden bleachers aren't particularly comfortable when all that separates you from splinters is a thin, cotton panty.

She couldn't tell if the midshipmen liked her sitting among them rather than jumping around on the field, but she was glad to hear Tim bellow in the stands several rows above her. One of his friends even used a bullhorn. On the whole, she thought the naval academy spectators sounded like a bigger crowd than they actually were. When you play the huge, local high school, size really does matter.

The midshipmen lost, of course, 35-10.

As she followed the crowd from the bleachers, Suzette noticed a group of local boys outside the field in the dirt parking lot, glowering at the girls as they walked past. Her mother and the cheerleading sponsor, Bunny Phillips, followed rather closely as the squad headed for their cars.

"We heard rumors that the Sanford boys wanted a fight," Mom said when they got home. "Your father was afraid things might turn ugly, so he asked the coaches to get the boys on the bus as soon as possible. Why in the world would they be angry when they won the game?"

Janice's face suddenly popped into Suzette's head.

She had an idea, but she wasn't sharing it. Not yet.

CHAPTER 13
Sideboy

"I'm hungry."

Dougie smiled in the darkness. His roommate always got hungry at night.

Dougie did, too, but the Mess Hall closed after dinner, and since midshipmen weren't allowed to have food in their rooms, that didn't leave many options.

So Dougie created one. Not bad for a freshman.

He "borrowed" the key to the pantry during breakfast one morning. The kitchen staff unlocked metal gates when they arrived and left the pantry open until dinner was served. During one free period, Dougie walked to the hardware store downtown and smiled earnestly at the clerk who copied it for him.

After replacing the original, he tucked his key in a foot locker and waited for a moment like this.

He sat up, clicked on a lamp, and grinned at his roommate.

"Let's get something to eat."

The boy stared as Dougie held out a shiny, silver key.

"Time for a raid on the galley."

"Where did you get that?"

"The helpful hardware man," Dougie said, pulling on his uniform pants and sneakers.

The roommates heard a soft knock on their door.

"Hey, you up?"

They exhaled and opened the door. It was Big Mac.

"I saw the light under your door. Hey, are you going somewhere?"

Dougie lunged for the lamp and turned it off.

"We're grabbing a bite to eat. Want to come?"

"Sure, where?"

"The galley."

They slowly opened the door and surveyed the darkened hallway. The entire football team was housed in the rooms that lined it.

The coach's room was at the end of the hall—the last door before the fire escape exit. Old, wooden floors seem to creak loudest at night, in the silence. If they were caught, the coach would definitely pull out the discipline paddle and worse—work them to death on the practice field.

They debated about heading down the main staircase to the Quarterdeck but decided it would be impossible. The rent-a-cop would see them long before they reached the kitchen.

The fire escape was their only option.

"Don't breathe, and don't sneeze," Dougie warned, tiptoeing down the hall. He hugged the wall opposite the coach's room and thought he heard faint snoring coming from inside. Each time a floorboard groaned, Dougie stopped. If the coach appeared, he simply would claim he wasn't feeling well and had been heading to the coach's room to tell him. He made a mental note to walk the hall during the day and plot a path with the fewest creaks.

After what seemed like an eternity, Dougie reached the exit door. Slowly, he turned the knob and pushed gently… nothing. He could hear his friend starting down the hallway.

He pushed harder, but it still didn't open.

"What the…?" Dougie whispered, breathing hard.

It's an emergency exit. It has to open, the boy thought, lowering his right shoulder and heading for the door like an opposing tackle at the five-yard line. It groaned as it swung wide, hurling Dougie into the wrought-iron railing on the fire escape.

The boys froze, waiting for their coach to emerge and kill them.

Miraculously, he did not.

They continued down the iron stairs and walked around the building to the one kitchen door that always remained open. They knew the rent-a-cop used it throughout his shift and had seen the kitchen staff enter when they arrived at six o'clock each morning.

Glancing around the empty Mess Deck, Dougie headed for the kitchen while his roommate peered down the hallway that led to the Quarterdeck.

"I saw the guard sitting in a chair, reading the newspaper," the boy reported. "We're clear for at least twenty minutes."

The pantry shelves stood behind old metal gates, and Dougie quickly slipped his key into the lock. Big Mac grabbed an enormous bin of cereal and a bowl as another opened the commercial cooler and helped himself to a fistful of luncheon meats.

"My man, you are a genius," he said, lifting a handle on the milk dispenser.

Dougie smiled.

They munched quietly until his roommate said, "That rent-a-cop makes rounds every hour, so we better wrap this up before he joins us."

The boys rinsed and replaced their dishes before Dougie locked the pantry gates. The three crept around the building until they reached the fire escape.

"Remember, that old wooden door sticks, so be careful," his roommate cautioned.

The wrought iron stairs wobbled silently as they climbed to the second floor. Dougie braced himself with one arm on the building and tugged on the door handle. It opened easily this time.

Their eyes remained focused on the coach's door as they slipped past and down the hall. The boys didn't exhale until they locked their own door, flopping on their bunks without removing a single article of clothing.

After tucking the key back in its hiding place, Dougie patted his full stomach.

He'd never slept better.

CHAPTER 14
Chain Locker

"I'm looking forward to seeing this concert," Mom said as she cleared the dinner dishes and Skipper watched for scraps. "Your father got those rifles donated by the department of the Navy."

"I get the band part of the concert, but what exactly is a drill team?"

"It's a marching unit that performs routines based on military drills. I've seen unarmed drill teams before that use flags, but the midshipmen will be armed."

"Oh, great. I hope the rifles aren't loaded."

Later, Suzette sat in the gym bleachers and watched as the guys tossed rifles back and forth, even spinning them in the air like batons. The midshipmen executed both marching and stationary routines with incredible precision. Rifles rolled across their shoulders, rested at their sides, and then dropped to tap the ground before bouncing back into their arms. She wondered how long they had been practicing.

"Those boys really put on a show," said her mother, clapping loudly.

They walked outside and headed across First Street to the main academy building. A handful of midshipmen strolled with them. There had been no Study Hall tonight, just a nice diversion, watching their classmates perform.

"Even the band sounded good."

"That's no small feat considering they were playing in a big old gymnasium."

Suzette stopped abruptly in the middle of the street, and her hands flew to her face.

"I can't see out of my left eye. Did I lose a contact lens? Is it stuck to my cheek? Please, don't anybody move or you might step on it."

Four pairs of eyes studied her face in the darkness and saw... nothing.

"I didn't do anything, Mom. I swear, I just blinked."

Their feet stayed rooted in place as they squatted above the black asphalt in the dark.

"Not very much light, huh?"

"I wish this had happened right under the street light." Suzette felt like crying, but that would only make her vision worse.

"I'll watch for traffic. Getting hit by a car won't help us find your contact."

"The headlights might help, though."

"My eyes were a little dry sitting in the gym, but I've never had a lens just pop out before."

It usually required pulling on the outer edge of her eyelid to get them out. It was bad enough that she would have to order a new lens. Worst of all, the Captain would be proven right. Even if it was a weird accident, Suzette had lost one of her contacts, and it would cost money to replace it. She and her mother would never hear the end of it.

"Is this it?"

Dougie was grinning and holding a tiny circle of glass on the tip of his index finger.

"God bless your eyesight," said Mom, giving him a hug.

The group could finally move their feet without fear of crunching a contact.

"I'll drown it in cleaning solution when I get home."

76

Suzette kept her cleaning and wetting solutions by her bathroom sink and meticulously closed the drain whenever she used them to prevent a slippery little lens from disappearing down it.

She looked at Dougie.

"Thanks. You're forgiven... for cleaning out that air conditioning ductwork above my bathroom."

He blushed.

⚓

Debbie and Janice were bored. Despite the fact that it was Friday night, there was nothing to watch on television and no parties or games to attend.

"Let's go to the Dairy Whip. I could use a hot fudge sundae."

Debbie picked up the keys to her mother's station wagon. At eleven at night, the streets of downtown Sanford were deserted. She drove slowly, obeying the twenty-five-miles-per-hour speed limit that frustrated her during the day. Most of the shops were closed. Just a couple of bars and the pool hall were still open.

"Who are they?"

The girls spotted four guys waving from the side of the road.

"Wait a minute—isn't that the guy they call The Menacer from the naval academy?"

"Yeah, but he's not wearing a uniform. Neither are any of the others. Wow, they look so different in civilian clothes."

The girls pulled the car over to the curb and rolled down the windows.

"We signed out for liberty this weekend, but we don't have any place to go."

Janice started laughing.

"That wasn't real smart."

"Yeah, don't rub it in."

"Can we come to your house?"

Debbie blinked. "Well, I'd have to ask my folks if it's okay."

The Menacer slid into the front seat next to Janice while the others piled into the back of the station wagon. They cruised over the ancient brick streets with the windows down and a cool, night breeze blowing their hair.

"Sorry, we didn't recognize you out of uniform."

"Too hot to handle, huh?"

"That must be it."

"Think your parents will mind having us stay over?"

"I don't know—they were in bed when we left."

Debbie parked in the driveway of her parents' wooden, one-story cottage. Moonlight peeked through the canopy of oak trees as she opened the screen door and motioned for the boys to follow her inside.

"I'll be right back," she whispered.

They sat in the living room, waiting in an uncomfortable silence.

"I guess we can always sleep in the station wagon," The Menacer offered.

"Y'all don't be silly. Debbie's mom is so sweet. She'll let y'all stay."

Moments later, the woman appeared in a bathrobe carrying an armful of blankets. Debbie hurried behind her with pillows.

"I hope you boys don't mind sleeping on the floor. One of you might take the couch, I guess. We just don't have enough beds in this house."

Laughing, they chose their spots in the living room. Janice and Debbie said goodnight and disappeared down the hall to Debbie's bedroom.

"It's kind of like camping but better."

"Yeah, no snakes or bugs," one said, yawning.

It might have been the sound of bacon sizzling in the pan, or it might have been the aroma, wafting through the air, which woke the boys. Either way, The Menacer thought his stomach was growling so loudly it could be heard in the next county.

"Good morning, boys. Are you hungry?"

Debbie's mother was beating an enormous bowl of pancake batter as Debbie poured orange juice into a row of glasses.

"Yes, ma'am."

"Wow, something smells good."

They slid into chairs around the kitchen table, and Debbie's mother said they looked happy as a flock of seagulls with a bag of French fries.

"Does anyone want coffee? I'll make some if y'all will drink it."

Janice stood beside the coffee pot with her hand on her hip.

"I'll have a cup—thanks," said one, scratching his head.

"Um, may I please have a glass of milk?" The Menacer asked.

Pancakes and syrup were passed around the table as Debbie's mother stood over the griddle and cooked more. She loved hearing the boys' laughter and her daughter's giggles. She felt sorry for the midshipmen's families, who missed so much by sending their sons to boarding school. She was happy they made themselves at home in her kitchen.

"Why do small tables always lead to big conversations," she wondered.

When they threw up their hands and insisted they could eat no more, she poured herself a cup of coffee and pulled up a chair at the table.

"We really appreciate you letting us spend the night," The Menacer said. "Our plans for weekend liberty kind of evaporated, and the local guys, well, they don't seem to like us very much."

He shrugged.

Debbie's mother nodded and patted The Menacer's arm. "Boys, it's much easier to judge people than it is to understand them. Understanding takes patience. Remember that."

"Yeah, I guess."

One boy filled the sink with soapy water and washed the dishes, which another dried before Debbie and Janice stacked them in the cabinet.

"You boys are good house guests, and you're welcome back here any time."

She hugged each of them before they walked to the car.

Debbie smiled.

"I'll be back home as soon as I drop them off at the academy, Mom."

Suzette enjoyed listening to the radio.

If an annoying song came on, she simply pushed a button and listened to something better on another station. The problem with vinyl record albums was if you bought one because you liked a single song, you were stuck listening to a bunch of other stupid ones along with it. That seemed like a colossal waste of time to Suzette and the main reason why she never bought many albums.

The second reason was because she had nothing to play them on.

She was criticized soundly for it. The few boys allowed in her room all inquired about her stereo. They were disappointed to learn that she didn't own one and offered advice on what she needed to purchase. She listened to a long lecture about JBL speakers from one only minutes before another boy insisted Panasonic versions were better.

"I would go with a Pioneer SX-727 Receiver with a Dual turntable and Advent speakers," Tim offered, sipping iced tea at the kitchen table. "You just have to make sure your speakers can handle all those amps so you don't blow them out when you crank it up."

Her mother—carrying pizza boxes from the delivery guy at the front door—raised an eyebrow. "I don't think she'll be cranking it up too much, Timmy."

Suzette noticed he had been spending several afternoons talking to her mother, and she always seemed to arrive in the middle of their conversations.

Tim grinned at her. "What's that?"

He nodded toward a clothing bag hanging on the door. A pantsuit had just been purchased for the homecoming game and dance at Our Lady of Perpetual Guilt.

"Why don't you try it on with the shoes you'll be wearing, and I can pin up the hem of the pants?" Mom asked.

Suzette obeyed.

When she had emerged from a dressing room at the store, her mother's eyes lit up. Suzette had come to appreciate this non-verbal method of evaluating her wardrobe: If Mom's lips were pursed and her head cocked to one side, the outfit looked bad.

In this case, an aqua turtleneck sweater with an ivory jacket and pants made Suzette's blue eyes pop in a "virginal queen" kind of way.

Tim stopped chewing. "You're wearing that to a football game?"

"Yes, I'm *watching* the game, not playing in it."

He laughed. "I know, it's just…white."

"Winter white," she corrected.

"Well, it looks nice."

"Thank God I have your approval."

Actually, Suzette was glad. Tim's opinion was sort of a barometer for guys, in general. If she passed inspection with him, others would approve. He was always honest and looked out for her like the big brother she never had. He became kind of her litmus test, easy to read and definitely better looking.

She would have preferred to wear a dress to homecoming, but she was double dating with Julie, who had chosen a pantsuit. A quiet girl whose last name placed her in Suzette's alphabetized home room, Julie moved to Florida from New Jersey a year earlier than Suzette. Yet even after attending eighth grade in town, Julie still didn't fit in.

"We're different, you know, from the kids who have lived in Florida all of their lives," Julie said matter-of-factly. "They even speak a sort of Southern dialect that leaves us out, entirely."

Suzette laughed. Julie was right. As military offspring, they both had lived in other cities, experienced different cultures, and made new friends every time their families moved. Kids who started kindergarten together and continued in the same classes through high school had their own kind of code that developed from years of shared experiences. They didn't need or want newcomers. They shared teachers, activities, and history, like an extended family.

Suzette was glad that Julie sat behind her in most of their freshman classes and rode the same bus home. They were kindred spirits even as they stood under the pine trees in a dirt parking lot waiting for the bus. While other buses lined up along the curb at the end of each school day, the one from Sanford arrived late and parked in an unpaved lot.

"I worry about getting chiggers from all these pine needles while we stand here waiting," Julie said, glancing at the ground. "Did you know they're members of the arachnid family, and they live in tall grass in wooded areas?"

"No, but I think you need to pay less attention in science class," Suzette said, looking down. "Why don't we walk across the street and get a Popsicle?"

The girls had learned that eating something icy cold somewhat mitigated the heat they endured during the long ride home. As they enjoyed their frozen treats, Julie talked about the homecoming dance.

"That guy from the JV baseball team asked me to go with him," Julie had confided earlier at lunch while eating her peanut butter, marshmallow, and banana sandwich.

The shortstop also was the class clown. Physically, he was more mature than the rest of the ninth-grade boys. He was able to grow full sideburns and was shaving every day, but the guy was a comedian—always seeking the limelight—and the first to try out for the school talent show.

Occasionally, his flair for the dramatic benefitted everyone. Suzette remembered when he brought a huge birthday cake to school for their first-period English teacher. The woman was old enough to be their grandmother and was so delighted by the cake and candles, she forgot to give the scheduled grammar exam, abandoned her lesson plans, and spent the entire hour slicing and serving her cake. Of course, nobody knew when her actual birthday was, but the class sung a rousing rendition of "Happy Birthday" at the top of their lungs, and she beamed.

As a diversionary tactic, it was brilliant.

"You should go to homecoming," Suzette said, earnestly. "We're freshmen, and it's an honor to be asked."

"Well, the shortstop mentioned that his friend wants to take you. We could double, and, Suzette, it would be so much more fun if you were with me."

Suzette blinked.

Go with a JV catcher, the shortstop's sidekick?

At least he was taller than Suzette. Unfortunately, the catcher's dark hair usually looked like it hadn't been washed, and rampant acne erupted on his face. He was perhaps the only ninth-grader who hadn't discovered Clearasil or a dermatologist.

Still, he seemed intelligent in class, and he didn't talk a lot.

"C'mon, Suzette; say you'll go with him. It's just dinner, a dance, and a football game…, and *we* get to pick the restaurant!"

Suzette started to laugh. It was a pretty good argument, and she really did like Julie. It was kind of a relief to have a friend who, like her, was in the process of finding her place in the school pecking order.

"Okay, sure. I'll go with the catcher. Well, with *you*, actually, but he can buy my dinner."

Sometimes Suzette regretted not doing very much at her own high school because she spent most of her free time at the naval academy. Since the catcher worked up the courage to ask, she thought it might be nice to participate in something social. Everyone was talking about homecoming anyway, at lunch and after classes, so at least she could be part of the discussion.

Unfortunately, at Our Lady of Perpetual Guilt, there was virtually no crossover between grades: freshman girls do not date senior boys. Freshmen date freshmen. Period. Suzette figured there was probably something written about it in the handbook after "ankle socks."

She faced no such discrimination as a cheerleader at the academy. She could hang out with seniors who drove without

84

their parents, and, frankly, she found them to be a lot more interesting.

In the interest of having friends where she attended school, Suzette decided to give homecoming a shot. She wanted to fit in, and this was a start.

Suzette must have dozed off because the sound of voices outside her bedroom door jolted her awake with a Spanish book still opened across her chest.

"It's really lovely." Mom was gushing at someone. It was the tone of voice she used when she didn't know someone very well.

Suzette rolled out of bed and carried a yawning Skipper into the hallway. Tim stood there with a pretty, platinum blonde whom she recognized from pictures as his girlfriend. Her tanned left hand was extended, and Mom was admiring the diamond ring on it.

"Come look at the engagement ring Tim gave his fiancée."

It was lovely, but it should be: Suzette remembered hearing that the platinum blonde's mother owned a jewelry store. Tim stood tall with his shoulders back, and his face flushed with pride. Suzette knew he wore only a high-school military uniform, and he was nineteen years old, but at that moment, he seemed so much older, like an adult who just made a life-changing decision.

She barely knew what she wanted for breakfast.

"Wow. Congratulations!"

So, this was what Tim had been discussing with her mother. Suzette sort of remembered hearing that the platinum blonde was older and looking for a commitment. Tim probably was looking for some stability after graduation. He would be headed for work in his father's citrus groves instead of college.

It dawned on Suzette that Tim probably thought of her as such a little kid. Mom invited them to have a seat in the living room, but Tim shook his head.

"We can't stay. We just wanted to show you the ring before she heads back home."

He hugged her mother tightly, and, for once, Suzette didn't mind sharing. Tim seemed to need her approval, but, of course, he had it.

Surprisingly, Suzette felt a tiny bit of sadness at the news. She wasn't quite sure if her expanding sense of family just added a new member...or lost one.

CHAPTER 15
At Ease

"I love Halloween."

Joey Perkins carefully hung orange, paper pumpkins around the Mess Deck with Suzette. Bunny Phillips begged for their help with decorations after school.

"I remember planning my costumes for weeks when I was a kid," he said grinning. "We'd fill up great big pillowcases with candy when we went trick-or-treating around our neighborhood."

"I kind of miss my mom this time of year," he added, swatting at a paper pumpkin. "She loves sitting on our front porch, watching the neighborhood kids come by in their costumes."

He perched on a step ladder waiting for Suzette to cut a piece of clear tape.

"She and my aunt drove me to Sanford from Brunswick, Georgia, to look at the naval academy one summer," Joey said. "A guy in my hometown was already enrolled here, and he brought me a pamphlet from the school. It was the only way my mom knew to get me away from my abusive old man. She works every day at Southern Bell to pay my tuition, here. Once, she even crossed a picket line to go to work."

Suzette looked up at Joey. His mother sounded like an amazing lady who worked to pay for her son's safety.

"Maybe I can to meet your mom sometime? Next time she visits."

Joey nodded, happily.

"Did you know every year on Halloween, they show horror movies on the Mess Deck to keep us out of trouble?" he asked. "A few upper classmen sneak out to go trick-or-treating, of course, but they always make it back for 'Taps' at ten o'clock."

"Really?" Suzette blinked. "I'm not big on horror flicks, but thanks for all your help with the pumpkin decorations. Looks like we're done."

Joey folded the ladder and carried it to the maintenance closet before heading upstairs to his room.

"It's a shame the rent-a-cop has to spend his Halloween in here with us," he said to his roommate.

"Yeah, he could use a treat."

Joey's roommate yawned in his bunk as Joey rolled over and stared at him.

"You're so right, and I've got something in mind," he said.

Joey opened the footlocker at the end of his bed, pulled out a bag of balloons, and tossed one onto his roommate's bed.

"Blow that up."

Joey twisted a wire hanger into an oval loop and tied the balloon to the top. Then he tore the brown wrapping paper off the package of fresh laundry that was recently delivered to their room and grabbed a white sheet.

His roommate watched, fascinated.

With a black marker, Joey drew eyes and jagged teeth. He threw the sheet over the balloon and attached a pulley at the top. Slowly, he opened their bedroom door and looked into the hallway. It was clear.

"Go to the end of our wing and watch the main corridor, okay?"

Joey carried a desk chair into the hall and stood it under the fire sprinkler. Quickly, he looped clear fishing line over the sprinkler head, hurried to the other end of the hall, and repeated it on a second sprinkler head just in front of the emergency exit. Then, he ran the monofilament over the emergency door and out to the fire escape. His roommate handed the "ghost" on the pulley to Joey, who added a slipknot before tying the line to the door handle.

The pair grabbed the chair, scurried back to their room, and waited, panting in the darkness.

Sometimes they could actually smell the rent-a-cop before they could see him. The distinctive odor of tobacco wafted a few feet ahead of him as he walked. His route was fairly predictable. Around eleven o'clock, he took a key that was chained to the wall at the end of their wing and turned it in the time clock box that he wore on a strap over his shoulder. That simple procedure recorded the exact time he made rounds each evening.

Tonight—as he did every night—he also opened the exit door and peered into the fire escape. That's when the "ghost" dropped down on the pulley and shot down the hallway toward the main corridor.

A high-pitched howl pierced the silence, followed by heavy footsteps thundering down the wooden floors, and the jingling sound of key rings hanging from the man's belt added musical accompaniment.

Joey clapped a hand over his mouth to keep from shrieking with laughter. When the noise subsided, he crept into the hall and unhooked the ghost from its pulley.

"Wish we'd set up a camera," his roommate snorted, as he popped the balloon and stuffed the sheet into the closet.

"I may just major in engineering in college," Joey mused as he climbed into bed. "Man, this was the best Halloween ever."

He figured his mom would've liked it, too.

CHAPTER 16
Boat Hook

Suzette slid into her jeans and pulled on a red knit top that laced at the neck.

Who knew that drive-in movies still existed? Only in this two-cow town.

The midshipman who was picking her up seemed like a nice guy. He hadn't spent any disciplinary time in the Captain's office, so her parents gave their tacit approval to the date. The guy had hung around after pep rallies for weeks, waiting to talk to Suzette and the other cheerleaders; all knew him. She couldn't remember what position he played on the team...definitely not the quarterback. That was the cheerleading captain's boyfriend.

He had broad shoulders, a nice smile, and deep brown eyes rimmed with the darkest lashes she had ever seen. When he finally worked up the courage to ask Suzette if she wanted to catch a movie, she happily said yes. It's just that there wasn't much to do in Sanford, other than the old drive-in. She didn't care whose car he borrowed. Maybe he had his own hidden nearby— a lot did. If you knew a "townie", you could park your car at their house, as long as you didn't get caught using it during the week.

Suzette thought this boy was one of those midshipmen who kept cars in Sanford because they drove home on weekends. A set of wheels provided an escape—if you trusted the "townies" not to mess with your car during the week.

He arrived at her door wearing jeans and a T-shirt, very impressive. Those muscles didn't show under the starched gray shirt and uniform pants he usually wore.

Civilian clothes looked better on him, definitely better.

The car wasn't bad either, with a gearshift and long bench seat instead of two buckets.

"You look nice."

"Thanks. So do you."

The silence was okay, but this could be a long night if she couldn't think of something to talk about. Suzette tried again.

"I'm glad there's no game tonight."

"Me, too," he said yawning. "I've got an English paper due Monday, so my weekend is spent."

Suzette nodded, but she really didn't understand why. She had seen some of the papers other seniors had turned in to the English professor and read them out of sheer boredom. In some cases, she edited them and had been amazed at the number of spelling and grammar errors. Suzette was even more amazed to later see that the midshipmen received "Bs" for their efforts since the same paper would've flunked her freshman English class.

Clearly, this boarding school had very different academic standards.

The boys talked freely about the professor, who also taught psychology and drama at the academy—heavy on the drama, actually. He wore a toupee that was as obvious to everyone around him as the bulbous nose on his face.

Suzette heard rumors that he invited students and their dates to his home on weekends, where beer and cocktails flowed freely. Of course, she was never invited. She was the Captain's daughter, and that might be risky if she shared details with her father. Most of the academy students were underage, after all.

"Do you think his head itches underneath that thing," Suzette asked.

Her date grinned.

"I've never seen him scratch it. I guess you could say he is challenged in the follicle department."

They parked and walked to the snack bar for popcorn and sodas, beneath a sky that was turning purple in response to the setting sun.

When they got back to the car, the midshipman opened her door in what Suzette assumed to be a devastating display of Southern manners. Instead of walking around to the other side, he slid in quickly beside her.

"I hate bumping into the steering wheel," he explained.

The popcorn tasted pretty good, actually. When the previews started, Suzette leaned back against his chest, and he raised his left arm to the seat above her shoulders. He smelled like soap mixed with cedar chips, warm and woodsy. In the middle of a graphic war scene—why do guys always want to watch people being blown up?—she caught him staring at her instead of the screen. Then, ever so slowly, he leaned in and kissed her. He tasted salty, and his tongue licked a drop of melted butter off her chin.

A nice smile and a great kisser—bingo! Her insides did a little dance.

She slid into his chest until he held her, like a baby, across his lap with their feet practically touching the driver's door. Explosions on the movie screen burst from the speaker hanging in the car window. Suzette trembled though she couldn't tell if a sound effect from the movie or the strength of his arms was causing it. In between kisses, the roughness of his chin rubbed across her lips until they burned. He kissed her again, and a jolt of electricity shot from her chest to her feet, tingling a number of areas in between.

Suzette now fully grasped the literary romance term, "It made my toes curl."

She opened her eyes and discovered she couldn't see the movie screen. The windshield had steamed up.

His mouth settled on her neck, and she felt the warmth of his breath as his hand gently squeezed her right breast. She froze, suddenly unsure of her ability to control the muscular athlete making out with her. He was bigger, stronger, and moving toward an intimacy that made her very uncomfortable. The amazing, romantic feelings stopped as suddenly as they started, replaced by a rising sense of alarm. She thought about Janice and wondered if her friend had parked at this drive-in, too.

Immediately, Suzette pulled away and sat up.

"Hey, what time is it?"

The clock on the dashboard blinked ten thirty, and she knew they had better get going if she was going to make her eleven o'clock curfew.

"I've gotta go."

For once, Suzette was glad that her bedroom was next to the front door. She could slip in without passing her father in the recliner.

His eyes usually gave him away. If the lids were red and lowered, she knew to avoid any interaction. In this house, "out of his sight" means "out of an argument." Her Mom once accused him of having eyes "at half-mast." She got points for the nautical reference, given where they live.

Okay, he's working at a boys' boarding school and not flying planes off aircraft carriers anymore. Does the whole family have to be miserable because of his career choice?

Get over it. There should be a statute of limitations for war heroes.

Occasionally, people told Suzette—well, adult women, anyway—how good-looking her father was. "Like a movie star," they said, and she remembered hearing that when he and some

Turner Classic Movies guy called Tyrone Power flew together in the Navy, their ship mates couldn't tell the men apart.

Suzette just couldn't see it. She never found mean guys very attractive. She was able to at least brush her teeth in the bathroom before she heard the soft tapping at her bedroom door. Of course, her mother wanted to hear all about the evening. Suzette told her a lot about the movie and a little about the boy, intentionally avoiding prying questions. It was none of Mom's business, and Suzette was feeling a bit worried about his real intentions. Maybe she needed advice from one of the older girls on the squad.

As she got ready for bed, she admitted to herself that she found the guy a little frightening. Her Catholic-school boundaries always seemed so simple: Don't have sex until you're married. Just don't do it, but it's much more complicated than that because there is a lot more physical stuff happening between kissing and sex. She knew that she needed to decide where her "line" was before she got into a compromising situation. The last thing she wanted was to end up doing something she would regret, simply because she didn't think ahead.

Robbie Sherman slid into the backseat next to Debbie and kissed her cheek.

"TGIF," he grinned.

"I have to warn you, my gas tank is almost empty," said the girl behind the wheel. "We can't go far when the little arrow is pointing to the big E."

Both Robbie and another midshipman pulled bills from their pants' pockets.

"Let's go to the gas station right now and put in a few bucks. Thanks for driving."

"Hey, I didn't have other plans. I'm up for anything. My parents trust me with the car." She smiled.

Debbie was glad her friend wanted to take a ride on a Friday night. Robbie's friend had no plans for the weekend, either, and asked to tag along.

Debbie hadn't found any movie listings that looked interesting, and at seventeen, the group was too young to get into a dance club and listen to music. There really wasn't anywhere to go—other than the old Sanford pool hall downtown—where alcohol was served, and ages weren't checked. They had Suzette in tow because, honestly, Debbie didn't mind her, and she figured Suzette needed to get out more.

"Anybody feel like driving to Orlando and paying our esteemed English professor and his toupee a visit?"

Professor Toupee lived alone, and as far as anyone knew, had never been married. He was cool and understood the boys' need to have a safe place to chill, so he maintained an "open-door policy" for midshipmen on the weekends. They were always welcome at his house.

Minutes later, the group cruised along the Interstate highway, with the windows open and the girls' hair flying. Academic stress and personal problems blew out of the car windows like empty gum wrappers. Every mile they drove farther from the academy, they felt relaxed—free. The midshipmen's disciplined lives disappeared in the rear-view mirror.

"Do you know where we're going? I mean, do you know the address?" the driver asked.

"I remember where it is. I've been there before," Debbie called from the back seat. "Take the Princeton exit off the Interstate."

They drove slowly along Mills Avenue, passing Lake Estelle Park. The speed limit was thirty-five, and Debbie remembered police cars often lurked on side streets, watching for speeders. They didn't need a ticket.

Professor Toupee's neighborhood was lined with large oak trees that hovered protectively over one-story ranch houses. Street names had an English flair: Nottingham, Norfolk, and Dorchester. Two cars were parked in front of his house and another in the driveway—which made it easier to spot. Jazz music drifted out of open windows that faced the street, followed by occasional bursts of laughter.

"You sure we can just drop in?"

"Are you kidding? His house is always open to midshipmen. He doesn't care how many people show up."

Robbie pulled Debbie from the car, and they headed to the front door. When it opened, they were surprised to see most of the sailing team sitting around the living room. Professor Toupee rose from a wing chair wearing a velvet smoking jacket and a shirt that was open at the neck.

"Are you hungry? Have you eaten?" he asked. "Make yourself a sandwich. I have a few things for you in the fridge."

The bottom shelf in the refrigerator contained neatly-stacked beer cans. Above them, sliced ham, cheese, and a leftover meatloaf looked amazing—practically a buffet.

Bags of chips and pretzels lay open on the counter, though more lined the coffee table next to bowls of dip.

"What would you like to drink? I have plenty of beer, of course, but I also have a bit of white wine."

The professor settled back in his chair and held court. Guys sat on the floor and the couch as they ate, laughing and joking like this was a fraternity party. Their host didn't mind hearing the occasional curse word and welcomed casual, civilian attire like

T-shirts and cut-offs. Suzette heard he even let midshipmen spend the night on weekends if they'd had too much to drink.

"Better to be safe than sorry," he would say.

Suzette plunged a potato chip into a bowl of dip and grabbed Debbie's arm as her friend walked by. She wanted Debbie's opinion about her drive-in movie date.

"Watch out for that guy," Debbie said, grabbing a chip. "One of the other girls on the squad told me he tore her blouse trying to rip it off her. All he wants is some action."

Suzette could feel her cheeks starting to flame.

"Are you okay?" Debbie asked, raising an eyebrow.

"Yeah, fine," Suzette answered. "Hey, what time do you need to get the car home?"

"Midnight, I guess. Oh, wow, we need to get on the road."

They steered Robbie toward the door, stopping to shake Professor Toupee's hand.

"That was fun."

Debbie rested her head against Robbie's shoulder as the car headed east.

The road back to reality stretched in front of them.

CHAPTER 17
Safe Haven

S uzette looked at her mother.

What did the woman do all day?

She had no friends in this tiny little town. They didn't even live in a subdivision where she might meet a neighbor on her way to the mailbox. God, there wasn't even a mall nearby.

Suzette suspected her mother spent most of her day mothering midshipmen. Evidence of Mom's growing popularity appeared in the form of gifts like the ceramic Christmas tree made by Big Mac's younger brother. Then came the earrings Dougie made from anchor insignias worn on his uniform.

Suzette sighed.

Her mother loved to talk on the phone. Suzette suspected that was a byproduct of being a Navy wife. If you only lived in a place for two or three years, how else could you stay in touch with the friends you made?

Suzette wrote cards to her friends from junior high school back in Boston but nothing like the missives her mother wrote to her friends. That woman scribbled pages and pages of letters at the dining room table in perfect Catholic-school penmanship.

At Christmas, it got worse. Handwritten notes were sent to hundreds of friends and acquaintances they had been stationed with. When Suzette said goodnight and went to bed, her mother was writing at the kitchen table. In the morning, she staggered out for breakfast and found Mom still at it, a pen and paper next to her cup of tea.

I'll never send Christmas cards, Suzette thought.

Some midshipmen got pretty creative in eating outside of the Mess Deck. They had their parents set up charge accounts with the Holiday Inn dining room, for example.

"My father told me to take my younger brother and maybe a friend or a roommate to dinner on weekends," Big Mac confided to Suzette. "I think he was afraid we might get sick of the food at school and wanted to give us another option. The hotel sends him the bill each month, which is great for me."

Others, like Joey Perkins, were helped by some of the school's younger staff members.

Several nights each week, he watched the clock.

With twenty minutes left before Study Hall break, he slammed his biology book shut and grabbed a notebook and pencil. After making the Honor Roll, he was allowed to study upstairs in his room rather than in the crowded Mess Deck.

Joey went door to door, jotting down orders and collecting cash. Just as the bell rang, he dashed downstairs to one of three pay phones on the front portico. He knew the number for Crusty's Pizza by heart.

When Study Hall ended, he jumped into the Chevy Vega hatchback belonging to a twenty-three-year-old House Father and headed downtown. He picked up twenty pizzas, carried the boxes up the fire escape, and distributed them. To save time, Joey always made sure that Crusty's wrote the midshipmen's room numbers on each order.

"Do you know who that underclassman was, the one who kept following me around?"

Joey asked his roommate as he peeled off a piece of pepperoni.

"Nope, but I did notice him leaving a few rooms carrying a slice of pizza. Bet he didn't pay for any of 'em."

Hundreds of people lined First Street in downtown Sanford for the annual Christmas Parade, which featured dozens of floats with politicians, animal rescue groups, dancers, classic cars, and, of course, Santa Claus.

Carolers serenaded the crowds as children ran around or tossed a football in the road, waiting for the parade to make its way up from its starting point in front of the naval academy.

A pair of police cars led the way with lights flashing and sirens blaring. Following them was a cadre of local politicians and veterans, middle school and high school cheerleaders. Finally, the Sanford High School marching band, which got the crowds moving with drum line-heavy versions of classic Christmas songs, appeared around the corner.

All of the midshipmen were lined up in formation behind the battalion staff. Suzette and the rest of the cheerleading squad chatted with the boys while waiting for a signal to move forward. They carried their pom-poms and were designated to walk ahead of the uniformed midshipmen, but just behind was an open convertible which was to carry the superintendent and the Captain.

Suzette's mother surveyed the scene as she stood beside the car holding a nervously shaking Skipper in her arms.

"I think little boys like to see the police cars, and little girls like to see the cheerleaders," she said.

The Captain climbed into the convertible's back seat.

"Oh, I think a few little boys like the cheerleaders, too."

The ghost of Christmas past haunts us all.

Suzette's early Christmas rituals occurred in a snowy city, with aunts and uncles, neighbors, and friends gathered at her grandparents' dining table. The scene was pure Norman Rockwell.

Norman Rockwell never painted this one.

When the school emptied of students during Christmas break, the Captain's nightly ritual of Cutty Sark—consumed in his reclining chair facing the television—drove Suzette and her mother out of their small apartment to search for something festive.

They found it in the lights on the twenty-foot tree which glowed brightly in the middle of a deserted Quarterdeck. Suzette liked to think the lobby of the original resort hotel probably had a similar one, but then, they probably had more guests to enjoy it.

Chairs in the far corners of the room disappeared in the dark, along with offices, classroom doors, and the stairway leading to the upper floors. Surprisingly, the illuminated area surrounding the tree seemed kind of cozy as her mother settled on one couch with Skipper and Suzette on another, basking in the Christmas lights.

When it came to enjoying holiday decorations at the academy, it was either a feast or famine, the small tree in their claustrophobic apartment or the enormous version in the deserted school lobby. Odd that both spaces felt equally empty to Suzette, lacking in the warmth that gives holidays their special meaning.

She knew that a Christmas tree alone does not constitute a holiday. That came in the form of the midshipmen, those young gentlemen-in-training, who arrived at her door in the evenings

101

under the pretext of questions for her father. In truth, she figured they needed her mother's attention more, along with some semblance of family life.

Suzette never considered herself to be an only child, yet the seven-year age gap between her sister, Michelle, and she made it seem so. She left for college when Suzette was in the sixth grade, and by the time the family got to Sanford, Michelle was living in Boston.

Magically, their apartment had filled with new siblings. A handful became regular guests at the dinner table since an invitation from her family provided a chance to escape the crowds and sameness that was served in the Mess Hall.

She guessed that midshipmen joined the family based on some combination of her father's opinion of them, her mother's intuition, and her own tolerance of their friendly overtures. They filled a void she scarcely knew existed, and suddenly, they were gone.

The Christmas tree was the last remnant of weeks filled with cookies, gift exchanges, and Big Mac's arrival as Santa at an ice-cream-and-cake party hosted by the academy for sixty children from the Methodist Children's Home. It provided a backdrop for photos during the Christmas Formal Dance where Suzette was escorted by a quiet, young man from Panama with soulful brown eyes. His courtly manners were a welcome change from the attentions of another midshipman from Charleston who had tried to woo her with weed. (Manners were important, especially when her mother and father—in his dress uniform—also chaperoned the dance.)

Those activities had lessened Suzette's "transplanted Yankee" loneliness and filled her with a sense of family far greater than the one she had been born into. The midshipmen needed the LeBlancs as much as the family needed them.

New rituals replaced her Norman Rockwell Christmas, yet tonight, Suzette couldn't shake the sinking feeling that she'd been jettisoned in favor of the boys' real holiday, the one spent with family members who shared their name.

Sitting in the empty Quarterdeck, mother and daughter wondered aloud about the midshipmen's homes, their parents and if the boys might miss them, too, when they returned to their native habitats.

"I bet Big Mac and his brother are cold in Connecticut."

"Yeah, the kids from New Jersey probably are freezing, too. The boy from Panama isn't too happy either since it's the rainy season there."

"Your sister said it was eighteen degrees in Boston when I spoke with her this afternoon. I'm sure she'll be glad to get on a plane for Florida tomorrow since the forecast is for seventy-five and sunny here."

"What are we going to do while she's here?"

"We can ride into Orlando and shop some of the sales. One day, we'll drive out to the beach and have dinner. Michelle has never seen the academy, and she'll probably be happy just to be through with college classes."

Suzette stared at the colored lights. She didn't want to go back to their apartment just yet.

"This tree is huge. I wonder where the school bought it."

"I don't know. We can ask your father. It really smells terrific though, doesn't it?"

They sat in silence for a while. Suzette wondered how her mother could live with a man who drank himself to sleep each night in front of the television. Both women missed the young men who had become such a part of their family until the boys joyfully abandoned them to return to their biological ones.

The temporary nature of those bonds became clear that night as the Christmas tree shimmered with blue and gold ornaments above "gifts" wrapped in shiny metallic paper.

Suzette knew the boxes beneath were as empty as her heart.

CHAPTER 18
Batten Down

Suzette didn't blame Robbie Sherman for choosing to stay in sunny Florida and spend time with Debbie instead of heading home to snowy Canada.

There were no other midshipmen left at school and no cheerleading practice for a month. The football season was over, and basketball season didn't start until next month.

She figured she might still see some of the girls—Debbie, of course, but Janice had mysteriously disappeared after her baby announcement. Someone said she had grown too big to hide the pregnancy, so her embarrassed parents demanded she drop out of sight.

A few girls who rode the bus to Our Lady of Perpetual Guilt with Suzette asked her about Janice. Well, they specifically asked who Janice's boyfriend was. They assumed it was one of the academy midshipmen and reported that the local guys weren't happy about it.

"Just be careful," one warned Suzette, as they walked together into class. "Janice's brother is really pissed at whoever knocked her up."

She didn't think it was meant as a threat, but Suzette felt very uneasy, especially after she found a note slipped into her algebra book. It was just one sentence scrawled on a sheet of lined notebook paper. "Get away from the anchor clankers. Go someplace safe for Christmas."

A warning?

Suzette wasn't thrilled with wearing shorts instead of her holiday sweaters, but when the sun lowered over Lake Monroe and a late afternoon breeze glided over the water, she had to admit the weather was pretty spectacular. Standing beneath an enormous oak tree draped in a shawl of Spanish moss, she listened to the crickets' serenade and watched Skipper stare at a squirrel on the tree trunk.

If it hadn't been so quiet, she might not have noticed the old sedan that slowed down as it drove past the academy. All four windows were open, so it was easy to see the guys inside who stared, and wait—did one of them just spit in the street?

"The natives are restless," she thought.

The phone rang later with an invitation that surprised her. Another freshman girl who rode the same bus called to say their local parish needed volunteers for the food pantry.

"That counts as service hours for us."

The academy was empty, and Suzette was feeling a little lonely. Mom even agreed to drive her there. As activities go, a food pantry was better than nothing.

Standing in front of the closet, Suzette waited for something to fall off a hanger—some kind of divine intervention or a sign. She had no idea what to wear to hand out canned green beans, and she wasn't going to make a big deal out of it by calling anyone who rode her bus to ask.

"Wear something with long sleeves, in case you get cold."

Mom loved wardrobe debates although she really didn't get a chance to participate in many since Suzette wore a school uniform most days.

"It also might be hot. How about these?"

She held up a fairly new pair of ice blue bell-bottom jeans and a sleeveless blouse.

In the car, they went through the verbal drill: Mom would pick her up at four o'clock unless she called sooner. The area around the church wasn't safe after dark, so she shouldn't walk anywhere. And for God's sake, she shouldn't put her Coke down anywhere because someone might drop drugs in it.

By the time she waved goodbye, Suzette felt like she could conduct a paramilitary operation on a small, communist country.

Inside the Fellowship Hall, she was surprised to see lines of people waiting to take a number and others seated in folding metal chairs. Long tables held rows of boxed doughnuts and biscuits next to bags of rice and beans.

The girls from the bus waved, so she headed for the safety of their circle. You'd think walking into a room full of strangers wouldn't bother her anymore. As a Navy brat, Suzette moved every three years and faced a new school..., Massachusetts, Pennsylvania, Louisiana.

Somehow, being "the new kid" never got any easier.

She was grateful for any welcoming smile and all attempts to include her. In fact, Suzette was so intent on making eye contact with each of the girls and signing in, that she totally failed to notice a god who appeared in their midst.

Long blond hair grazed his shoulders, and he wore a leather cord with a small shell around his neck. Suzette wasn't sure if his teeth were extremely white or his tan was extremely dark, but the combined effect was dazzling.

"Your first time here?" he drawled.

Suzette's mind raced. "He's asking me a question, and I better nod because words fail me."

He handed her an apron, and as they walked toward coolers filled with packages of frozen chicken, the people around them stepped back.

"Now I know how Moses' wife must have felt when he parted the Red Sea," she thought.

The gorgeous guy explained that people were given different packages of chicken parts, depending on the size of their family. She tried to memorize his instructions but was distracted by the fact that he was wearing the coolest Hawaiian shirt she had ever seen.

And the guy smelled even better than he looked! Maybe it was his shampoo or maybe it was his cologne. Maybe it was anesthesia because she could no longer feel her feet or her hands or any other part of her body. Suzette was floating.

When he finished explaining the Food Pantry rules, he apologized.

"Sorry, my name is Reef."

"I'm Suzette. Your parents call you Reef?"

He laughed, and his shiny white teeth blinded her.

"Yeah, they do now, but they called me Richard when I was born. That was before I learned to surf."

A surfer. Of course.

"I hear you go to Catholic School." Obviously, the kids who rode the bus with her had been talking.

"My parents' choice, not mine."

"Where do you live?"

"My dad is the commandant at the naval academy."

She hated saying it out loud because it sounded weird—even to her.

"You live there?"

He was staring at Suzette.

"Well, not with the midshipmen. My family has an apartment on the first floor."

He whistled softly.

"Bad news. Some dudes in this town really hate those anchor clankers."

She cocked her head, suddenly wary of Reef.

"Really, why?"

He lowered his voice to a whisper and leaned closer to her ear.

"One of 'em got my friend's sister pregnant. Not cool, you know?"

Suzette's mind started racing. He was talking about Janice.

Reef put his hands on her shoulders and looked directly at her with ocean-blue eyes that could melt the polar ice cap.

"You be careful, Suzette. There's some payback planned. It might get nasty."

Customers of the Food Pantry swarmed the table with their lists, but Suzette felt anxious. The next time she looked up at the clock on the wall it was only two o'clock, but she was ready to leave.

"I guess I'm not feeling quite as safe, anymore," she thought.

She woke the next morning with a start and then realized it wasn't a school day. She snuggled back under the covers, stretched, and savored the knowledge that she had all day to do nothing.

Mom appeared in the doorway just as Skipper jumped up on the bed.

"I'm going to the grocery store in ten minutes and running a few errands. Do you need anything?'

"Yeah, but I'll ride with you. I need some new hair stuff."

An hour later, Mom headed to Winn Dixie as Suzette walked next door into the only drugstore in downtown Sanford. She strolled along the hair care aisle, reading labels proclaiming, "Body builder, volume, thickening shampoo." She had no idea how long she'd spent engrossed in product ingredients, but when she headed for the cashier, Suzette noticed some guys on the hardware aisle who looked familiar. Janice's brother, Joe, had dropped her off at cheerleading practice a few times.

Her ears perked up.

"Look Joe, twenty boxes of matches. We all can carry some."

"Cool. They'll never see it coming. We gonna cook some squids tonight."

She paid for her hair stuff and ran to the car.

She needed to call Janice.

CHAPTER 19
Come About

Janice never answered the phone, and Suzette had no idea where she lived. Fortunately, Debbie did, so Suzette asked her friend to drive. They found the mother-to-be sitting on the porch, painting bright red nail polish on her toes when they arrived.

"But Janice, you have to tell your parents the truth about your baby's father."

She looked at Suzette oddly and answered slowly.

"Nooooooooo, I don't. They'll hate him before they even meet him."

Suzette shook her head. When did Janice start worrying about her parents' opinion?

She heard her own voice rising to a shriek, so she kept repeating to herself, 'Don't scream at her,' 'Don't scream at her.' She knew Janice would never fix things if she got mad.

"Your brother Joe and his friends need to know the truth, or they'll attack the school. They may burn down my house. Somebody is going to get hurt, Janice. You can't sit here and let that happen. You can't be that selfish."

Debbie put a hand on Suzette's arm to calm her friend, but it was shaken off.

"What is wrong with you, for God's sake?"

When she got to Janice's front door, Suzette shoved it open with such force she nearly knocked it off the hinges. She was worried that time was running out.

"God, I'm so confused and so scared right now."

Debbie hurried down the sidewalk after her, which was a good thing since she had the car and the keys.

"What are you going to do?" Debbie asked, nervously.

"Tell my parents or call the police. I haven't decided, but you and I can't guard the entire school tonight. It's too big, and it's too dark."

"Robbie will help us."

"Right, that would be three of us against how many of them? We don't have much of a choice here, Debbie."

She parked on the street—not too close to the building—and headed for the fire escape to get Robbie. Suzette sprinted toward her front door and saw the football coach silhouetted there, talking to Michelle and her parents.

She looked at the Captain to gauge his condition, and, for a split second, she felt relieved. He looked sober. His face wasn't flushed, and his eyes were wide open, probably startled by the sight of his daughter bursting out of the darkness.

"We've got a problem," Suzette gasped.

Words poured out of her in a furious torrent, like storm water after a hurricane. She told them everything about Janice, the pregnancy, the threats from Sanford boys. She was fighting to channel a calm and cool, just-the-facts-ma'am demeanor, but she was also trembling. Suzette had barely finished when Debbie and Robbie raced through the open front door.

"I'll call the police," the Captain said, grimly. "Coach, you patrol the south side of the property by the classroom building and take Robbie with you. Suzette, you and Debbie stay inside the building, but watch through the east windows toward the lake. I'll head to the north side by the Mess Deck. We're on our own until the patrol cars arrive."

Her mother locked their front door and picked up the dog.

"You did the right thing," she said, looking directly at Suzette. Then she headed to the Quarterdeck to keep an eye on the school's front entrance.

Suzette's heart was hammering so loudly she was pretty sure Debbie heard it, too. They peered out of rear windows overlooking the pool.

"Oh, God, oh God, oh God, oh God," she whispered mostly to herself. "How will we even know if they're outside...unless they're wearing headlamps?"

Figures crept along the building's outer wall, beneath darkened windows. The place looked deserted since spring break began, and the midshipmen were gone except for a couple of losers still stuck upstairs. One of the cheerleaders—Suzette—lived there with her family, but they lived in the only wing where lights still shone, so the boys avoided it.

The locals knew the school employed a rent-a-cop to patrol the property. They just didn't know if he carried a gun, so they avoided the front of the building because it was too well-lit. The side that faced Lake Monroe included a string of street lights, too.

Odds were pretty good they would not be discovered.

"Those squids sure will be surprised when they come back and find no school," Joe muttered. "Rich bastards with their fancy sports cars. They come here and think they can have anything or any girl they want."

His eyes narrowed, cold and hard. "Not any more. They can go home or go to hell. It don't matter to me."

Several of the others grunted in agreement. The anger that had smoldered for years was hungry for destruction.

A metal gas can carried by one, softly clanked against the baseball bat carried by another.

"Y'all hush," Joe said sharply. "I don't want no damn rent-a-cop out here."

They sprinkled gasoline in the grass along the building's foundation like a deadly trail of breadcrumbs for an invisible spawn of hell.

"The kitchen's on that side," Joe said, jerking his head to the right. "I saw the dumpster. We'll light it there. Somebody better go get the truck. We'll need to get outta here fast."

The crew slipped inside a sagging wooden fence, invisible to all but a passing seagull.

"We could break a window and throw the can inside to speed things up," someone whispered.

Joe paused to consider it. Not a bad idea. In fact, they could stack some tables and chairs and build a real bonfire. He pulled the matches out of his jeans pocket and looked up.

Standing in the arched doorway, Captain LeBlanc clicked on a portable searchlight.

"Is there something I can help you with, gentlemen?"

The flame in Joe's hand flickered in mid-air, just as the security guard rounded the corner with another boy squirming in his grip.

In front of the building, Janice and her parents parked under the portico. They saw Suzette's mother standing there, with Skipper tucked under her arm.

"Hello, Janice. These must be your parents?"

"Mrs. LeBlanc, I'm Janice's mother, and this is my husband. Our daughter just explained this terrible misunderstanding to us."

Her voice was drowned out by the piercing screech of a police siren, roaring into the driveway with flashing lights.

Suzette and Debbie bolted out of the front doors and almost collided with the group.

"Have you guys seen Joe, my brother?" asked Janice, her voice cracking as she struggled not to cry.

"No, we just saw the lights and heard the sirens and...."

Suzette lost her train of thought and stared at the front lawn where a small parade of boys was marching toward them, their hands behind their backs. They were led by a Sanford policeman, followed by the Captain and the rent-a-cop. The group all wore glum expressions.

Janice's parents hurried to meet them as the words "criminal trespassing charges" and "intent to commit arson" drifted through the night air.

Later, Suzette sat at the table in the apartment, holding Skipper's muscular little body in her lap. The dog snored faintly as Suzette clutched a cup of hot tea to steady her shaking hands. She was struck by the string of consequences that resulted from one bad decision. "Lying by omission," the nuns at Our Lady of Perpetual Guilt would say.

Janice didn't know any better, but her ignorance damn near caused a disaster.

She and her family would have to live with that, but so would everyone connected with the naval academy. The choices we make—both good and bad—have an impact on our future.

Suzette remembered reading a quote in English Lit class from the author Pearl S. Buck: "Every great mistake has a halfway moment, a split second when it can be recalled and perhaps remedied."

She hoped that she would be able to recognize those moments in her own life. Looking around the table, Suzette was surprised at how frightened she'd been at the thought of her home burning down. Her *home,* not just the academy. She felt connected to the place, for better or worse. It was where she belonged now. Her old life in Boston felt very far away.

CHAPTER 20
Breakwater

Michelle opened one eye and noticed the entire room was glowing. She could barely stand all the bright sunlight streaming through the windows and bouncing off of her white bedspread.

Disoriented until she spotted her suitcase on the floor, Michelle suddenly remembered that she was in Florida for the holidays, in a crazy boarding school that someone tried to burn down. She hadn't been able to see much of it last night, between the police and the teenage arsonists.

"Sorry about the light," said her mother, plopping Skipper down on the bed for a cuddle. "These window shades are pretty sheer, and I haven't bought any room-darkening drapes for this room yet. You haven't been here, so I didn't bother."

True enough.

Michelle was living with her grandparents while earning a degree at Massachusetts College of Fine Art. There was very little space between the old houses, and that meant very little sunlight ever reached her room.

Michelle had to admit it was nice to have her parents in Florida during the winter. She stretched and wondered how close they were to a beach. Surely, Suzette would know.

Her mother turned to a persistent knock at the door just outside Michelle's bedroom.

"Is the Captain available?"

A deep voice boomed from the hallway, and Michelle wondered if last night's policemen had come back. Suddenly, a head of dark curls appeared in her doorway.

"What's she doing in the rack?" a man asked.

"She's home from college and sleeping in," her mother said with a laugh. "Michelle, I think you met our football coach last night."

Michelle grinned and pulled one hand out from under the covers to wave.

"Is there a beach around here," she asked, stifling a yawn.

"Sure is. New Smyrna Beach and I'm heading there, myself, this afternoon," he answered. "It's about a thirty-minute drive, and after all the chaos last night, you deserve a nice day. Why don't you girls come with me?"

Michelle blinked and looked at Suzette. "What time?"

"After lunch. Or we could just grab a bite on the way if you'd like. I'm an excellent tour guide."

The coach drove a convertible. Its tiny size seemed in direct opposition to his girth, yet he slid behind the wheel without much effort and turned to Suzette and Michelle.

"You ladies might want to tie that up, somehow."

He pointed to their shoulder-length hair.

"Girls tell me the wind does terrible things to long hair. You don't want knots."

Michelle pulled a rubber ponytail holder out of her purse as Suzette yanked a baseball cap on top of her head.

"We're good."

About twenty minutes later, the coach pointed at New Smyrna Speedway.

"There's auto racing every Saturday night from the middle of March through December," he shouted.

Riding in a convertible certainly was noisy, Suzette decided.

They turned on historic Flagler Avenue, and the speed limit slowed as they drove past quaint shops and cafes. When they reached the beach, Michelle was startled by the sight of a bright blue sky over stark white sand.

"New Smyrna Beach is thirteen miles long, and you'll be pleased to know that it is consistently voted one of the Ten Best Beaches in Florida."

"Wow. They let you drive on it?"

"Yeah. You can drive along Daytona Beach, too. That's where Nascar started racing—on the beach. The sand here is a lot prettier."

Later, he parked beside a restaurant covered in weather-beaten shingles, and they sat beneath an umbrella overlooking the water.

"You girls need to try the fried grouper sandwich. It's a wonderful local delicacy and nothing like the cod you Bostonians eat."

"We also eat lobster," Suzette pointed out.

He grinned and ignored her.

"Just south of New Smyrna lies the Canaveral National Seashore, where you can swim, bird watch, hike, or whatever. Anglers at nearby Mosquito Lagoon have set international records with giant redfish catches.

"Deep-sea charters leave New Smyrna Beach daily, for offshore fishing in the Atlantic Ocean," he added. "Your dad might enjoy that."

Michelle thought she had never seen a more beautiful setting. It was vastly different from the rocky beaches where she played during summers on Cape Cod.

The football coach wasn't bad, either. He turned out to be quite intelligent and good at conversation, despite the fact that his personality was encased in a linebacker's body.

As they pulled up in front of the Academy, Michelle thanked him for being an excellent tour guide.

"When do you have to go back to college?" he asked.

Suzette rolled her eyes. The coach was obviously flirting with her sister.

"Maybe we can go listen to some music one night before you leave. I've got a friend who plays guitar in a local band."

Michelle smiled.

"Sure. That sounds like fun. And I'll be back in March for Spring Break."

CHAPTER 21
Cat 'O Nine Tails

When the midshipmen returned after Christmas break, they lugged suitcases upstairs to unpack. Tim was hanging starched uniform shirts in his closet when the battalion commander stuck his head through the bedroom door.

"Man, did you hear what happened while we were gone?" he asked. "I just got a haircut downstairs, and the barber told us a bunch of locals tried to set the school on fire."

"You're kidding, right?"

"I wish I was."

As word spread above decks and through the Mess Hall, midshipmen were shocked to learn of the attempted arson. Though several of the boys originally headed to Suzette's apartment to swap holiday vacation stories, the conversation ultimately turned toward the local tensions which nearly turned lethal.

Sitting on the living room floor with his back against the wall, The Menacer pressed the tips of his fingers together in what looked like a church steeple.

"I remember one Sunday night a couple of years ago when one of our underclassman came back from liberty crying," he said. "He got roughed up by some townies, so some of the upper classmen went into town and found who did it. I think they put a couple of them in the hospital."

"The upper classmen, who never said much about the younger kids, took matters into their own hands and made things right," he added. "That's pure brotherhood, not to mention pride."

Tim looked up from rubbing the dog's belly and tilted his head to one side. "Yeah, I kind of remember hearing something about that, too, but our guys didn't go burning any houses down."

He gave a low whistle and looked at Suzette. "That must've been hard for you. You kind of got caught in the middle, huh?"

"Yeah, I'm sure I made some enemies. Janice may never speak to me again. At least her brother is in juvenile detention now, so I won't be murdered."

"The rent-a-cop told me that you saved the school," Tim said. "If you hadn't called the police, this place would be a pile of ashes."

He locked eyes with Suzette. "That took guts. I'm proud of you."

He raised an arm to high-five her.

"Thanks," she said. "That means a lot."

The next morning, Suzette thought she may have actually levitated out of her bed.

She'd been dreaming that she was back in Boston, eating a hot fudge sundae at Brigham's Ice Cream Shop. Suddenly, music—loud, horrible…wait a minute; is that "Reveille"?

She flung off the bedspread and stood, blinking at a blind-folded boy with a bugle standing in the hallway outside her door. She glanced at the alarm clock on her nightstand. Six-thirty blazed in bright, red lights. That's when she heard their muffled laughter.

Suzette swung around the door frame and saw her mother with a demented smile plastered on her face. She was standing with two midshipmen who could barely breathe; they were laughing so hard. She wasn't sure which looked funnier, her disheveled self or a blindfolded bugler, who, by now, stood at attention.

"How'd you like the wake-up call?" Big Mac asked. "Your mom says you've been running late in the morning, so we thought we'd give this a try."

Suzette pivoted and slammed her bedroom door.

Happily, the school day passed quickly. It was a "holy day of obligation", so attending mass in the school chapel was mandatory for all students. Suzette noticed that the handshake normally exchanged during the "sign of peace" turned into back slaps, lingering hugs, intimate rubs, and, frequently, squeezes, during the service.

"I'm not sure these public displays of affection were exactly what the pope had in mind," Julie whispered.

"Really..., where is your sense of community? You don't see any couples locking lips, do you?" Suzette answered with a grin.

"Not yet...." Julie muttered.

Their final class of the day was gym, and for the past two weeks, they had been standing in a grassy field learning how to play softball.

"These polyester space suits are so itchy," Julie said, shielding her eyes from the blazing sun.

Mustard gold with a white pin stripe, the one-piece suit snapped at both shoulders and stretched, unattractively, over every other part of the body.

"Be honest. Have you ever seen anyone look good in this gym suit?"

Suzette thought about it as she swatted at a mosquito on her leg.

"No, actually... I haven't."

There had been one, tiny girl in their class who didn't have an ounce of body fat on her. Wearing the gold onesie, she looked like she could be in nursery school. Suzette didn't feel that "infantile" qualified as looking good. As soon as class was over, the girls peeled off their gym suits, pulled on their uniforms, and headed for the bus. No one ever showered after class, even if it was a hundred degrees in the shade. The girls at Our Lady of Perpetual Guilt were far too modest for getting naked in front of each other.

When she got home from school, Suzette wondered if the stupid bugler would be back. At least "Taps" would be a lot easier to take than "Reveille".

Many Orlando families owned condos at New Smyrna Beach. Suzette heard kids at school talking about trips there, so she was thrilled when Mary Grace invited her to spend a weekend.

"I also invited Julie to go, too. Mom asked me if I was sure I could handle entertaining two friends, but I told her we'd be fine. We can pick you up Saturday morning since the academy is kind of on our way to the beach."

Suzette was excited but also a little nervous. Why was making new friends always so hard? Every time her father was transferred and she moved to a new school, Suzette started the process all over again. Would anyone invite her to hang out? Would she have to eat lunch alone? Would she suffer through movies she didn't want to see, just to be included? Worst of all, would she be invited to go somewhere with a group only to be ignored once she got there?

Suzette learned to dismiss those thoughts and go anyway.

"You never can be sure how much fun something will be until you show up and see how it is for yourself," she rationalized.

Still, it could be damn exhausting.

But she liked Mary Grace and Julie. If conversation really lagged, they could always go for a swim, right?

Mary Grace's mother chatted with Suzette's mom in the academy driveway. By the time the car pulled away, Suzette was pretty sure that both women felt relaxed. Her mother was no longer worried that she might be unsupervised or abducted. If Mary Grace's mother thought living at a boys' boarding school was weird, she sure didn't show it.

Suzette didn't realize that she'd been holding her breath until the car pulled onto the Interstate, and she exhaled a long sigh of relief.

Thirty minutes later, the group carried grocery and overnight bags to a condo on the third floor of the building which, coincidentally, had three bedrooms. Two guest rooms were off the hallway by the front door. Mary Grace's parents' bedroom was off the living room, overlooking the water. A wooden dining table and chairs stood next to the galley kitchen. Nearby, a plump, ocean-blue couch was topped with oyster-colored pillows embroidered with starfish.

It was perfect.

Suzette and Julie were assigned to the room with twin beds. They dropped their belongings and walked into the kitchen where Mary Grace was sliding a pan of lasagna—lovingly made by her grandmother, Noona—into the oven. The three girls chatted easily as they chopped tomatoes, cucumbers and olives for the salad while waiting for the pasta to heat.

Food was such a wonderful common denominator.

Sliding glass doors in the living room led to a wide balcony, which overlooked a swimming pool and the sandy beach below. After dinner, the girls stretched out on chaise lounges on the balcony and listened to the seagulls as they sorted through shells they picked up on the beach. Suzette let the others do most of the talking and paid attention as they provided a bit of background on classmates she barely knew. She loved how easily the conversation flowed from one subject to another. That was the main difference being with girlfriends rather than guy friends. She didn't have to worry about hurting some guy's feelings. Even her most platonic relationships with midshipmen still had a little flirtatious edge to them. She guessed it was just the nature of the species.

Talking with Mary Grace and Julie was just so…relaxing. Yeah, that was it. Relaxing. She wasn't guarded, nervous, or uncomfortable. She was just…Suzette. They wanted her opinion—not stupid conversation just to try to get to second base. Even better, they were her age. These girls didn't drive—and didn't really date, either—so they couldn't make her feel completely juvenile and stupid. Instead, she felt totally at ease and accepted.

"Friends are kind of family you choose for yourself," she thought.

The wind off the water had picked up, and suddenly, Mary Grace's mother appeared on the balcony with three blankets. She had one for each girl to wrap herself in.

"Anyone want some hot chocolate? I was reading in my room, and I noticed the breeze seems to have turned cool."

The girls nodded and laughed. Suzette's own mother used to make hot chocolate a lot when she was little, but it was nice to be babied a bit, even now that they were grown up.

Suzette watched the moonlight bouncing on the waves. She pulled the blanket tighter and realized she couldn't remember the last time she felt so happy.

Mary Grace's mother carried four steaming mugs out to the balcony on a shiny, white tray. She sat down with the girls and held her own mug just under her chin to warm her hands. After a while, she turned to Suzette and smiled. It was as if she was reading the girl's mind.

"Sometimes the most ordinary things can be made extraordinary just by doing them with the right people," she said.

CHAPTER 22
Decks Awash

A half-hour's drive from Sanford, Walt Disney World opened with great fanfare. Many midshipmen hoped for a weekend bus trip, but when the Captain read about an upcoming "George Washington's Birthday Festival" at the theme park, he picked up the phone and made a pitch to the park managers. A few days later, he announced the Academy Drill Team would march in Disney's Main Street Parade and raise the American flag in front of Cinderella's Castle.

Mom thought it was a great idea.

"They'll look so handsome in their dress uniforms, and they get free admission to the park, too. You and I will go in our own car in case we want to leave before the bus does. Dad needs a few extra chaperones to keep an eye on the boys after they perform."

Fine. Suzette certainly had watched her share of military parades, so one more was no big deal. Besides, it was at Disney World, and she could skip school to go. Our Lady of Perpetual Guilt could go on without her for a day.

A Disney official met the group in the parking lot when the bus arrived. He didn't look much older than the midshipmen themselves, and he had a remarkably similar haircut. The guy was wearing a fitted blue jacket with a nametag that included mouse ears, though.

Suzette and her mother followed the midshipmen as the official led the group to a plain, boring door on Main Street USA. Suddenly, they were all underground in the biggest tunnel she had ever seen.

Hundreds of employees hurried past the group—some dressed like safari guides, ice cream salesmen, and Haunted Mansion maids or butlers. Cast members navigated the tunnels on foot or in battery-operated vehicles that looked like golf carts. Suzette actually saw the Mouse, himself, carrying his head under one arm. The guy was short, Asian, and very unimpressive.

"More than one million costumes are housed here, making it the largest operating wardrobe department in the world," the Disney guy informed them.

"These utility corridors are called 'utilidors', and the floor plan is a circle with a path down the middle. Tunnel walls are color-coded to make it simple for our cast members to determine their location." Hmmm. Suzette concurred that "cast member" was code for employee.

The utilidors were accessed from a main tunnel entrance located behind an area of the park known as Fantasyland or through unmarked doors—like the one Suzette and her mother walked through—which were located throughout the Magic Kingdom.

According to legend, since California got Disneyland before Florida got Disney World, there was time for changes. Founder Walt Disney didn't like seeing a cowboy walking through California Disneyland's Tomorrowland en route to his post in Frontierland. Disney thought it was jarring and detracted from the guest experience. When Disney World was built in Orlando, engineers designed "utilidors" to keep park operations out of guests' sight.

The utilidors may be under the Magic Kingdom, but they aren't a basement. (Suzette learned that a *basement* in Florida is generally called a *swimming pool*.) Because of an elevated water table, most of the tunnels were built at ground level. The Magic Kingdom was built above that. The guide explained that park guests like Suzette see streets that are elevated by one story and Cinderella's Castle actually sits at third-story-level, which explains why the castle appears large as you walk towards it down Main Street USA. The ground's incline is so gradual that you don't realize you're climbing to the second and third stories.

"The Magic Kingdom is built on soil removed from what is now the Seven Seas Lagoon," the guide said.

"Wow, that's pretty amazing."

As the midshipmen lined up for the parade, Suzette and her mother were escorted back out to Main Street USA. They searched for a spot in the crowd near the castle to stand and watch.

"I have to admit it; this is pretty impressive," Suzette murmured.

In their dress blue uniforms, tossing rifles and carrying swords, they looked like the real deal, dignified, military men, representing duty, honor, and service.

Suzette felt proud to be with them.

Maybe the fact that it was George Washington's birthday had something to do with it, or maybe it was because they were performing in the most patriotic, all-American place on the planet and not in front of jealous, judgmental boys from the town of Sanford.

At least no one called them "anchor clankers" all day.

The sailing team at the academy brought back more trophies than any other sport. That seemed logical to Suzette since it was a naval school. But the truth was, the guys worked hard at it, spending at least three afternoons each week on the water, racing across Lake Monroe.

In addition to developing sailing and racing skills, midshipmen learned boat and equipment maintenance, weather forecasting, and—most important—safety at sea.

Admissions brochures featured many pictures of Windmills, two-person sailing dinghies originally designed in 1953. The dinghy was inexpensive and could be built by amateur woodworkers like a father-and-son team or a pair of teenage guys. In addition to being simple to build and repair, the boats were fast and competitive, without the complexity of a spinnaker—a special type of sail—or trapeze—the wire that hooks onto a crew member's safety harness to keep him from falling into the water. Yes, Suzette had become a bit of an expert on such things.

The Captain talked about how easy the boats were to load on a trailer. He encouraged midshipmen to race in competitions since there were large fleets of Windmills in Florida. Owners traveled to regional regattas, which allowed the racers to see a lot of new places.

The sailing team loved working in the boat house. The smell of freshly-sawn wood was amazing. The guys mounted an oscillating fan on one wall to keep the place cool and eliminate paint and varnish fumes.

Suzette wasn't sure which the team loved more—the actual sailing or the time spent repairing the boats. Guys often pulled rotting plywood bottoms off the older models. Those were used as templates to cut and fit replacement pieces. Suzette once watched the boys attach new bottoms with wood screws and glue. The result was a lightweight yet strong, quick-to-construct hull.

"It's just like refinishing furniture," one midshipman said as he varnished the rails.

Suzette heard the team would be ready for The Royal Gaboon Race, which included boats of all sizes and crews of all

131

ages. It wasn't just a high-school sporting event—more of an "anything-that-floats" event. It sounded like fun, so some of the cheerleaders decided to attend and show their team spirit. Debbie convinced Suzette's parents to let their daughter go, too. They only let her go because Suzette's mom trusted Debbie, who always took time to talk with her and compliment new things Mom had done around their quarters.

"Your parents aren't worried because they know you're not dating anyone on the sailing team," she teased.

"True enough. I didn't think of that," Suzette said. "I also may have implied that your mother was coming with us."

"You're such a liar! Your dad and mom will kill me if anything happens to you."

The girls piled into Debbie's station wagon late Friday afternoon while it was still light and followed the academy truck as it hauled boats west to St. Petersburg. After stopping for hamburgers at a fast-food restaurant, they checked into their motel rooms.

The girls chose beds in their room and answered a knock at the door. Two midshipmen stood holding coolers, with the rest of the team standing behind them.

"Is anybody thirsty?"

They filled the bathtub with ice from a machine before adding a dozen bottles and cans.

"Want a beer?" one asked, looking at Suzette.

"Um, not a whole one. Maybe just half?"

"Great. That means there's more for me."

Suzette grabbed a plastic cup from the bathroom counter and held it as he poured. Her father had offered her a sip of beer once or twice. Suzette distinctly remembered that it tasted bitter. Actually, it tasted pretty terrible.

"Cheers."

Bottles clinked with her plastic cup. She took a sip. Ugh. The flavor was worse than she remembered. She held her breath so she couldn't really taste it and sipped again. That was a trick she learned as a kid from eating her sister's Swedish Meatballs. God, they were terrible. They originated from a recipe in the Betty Crocker cookbook for kids, and her mother had been thrilled when Michelle learned to make them. The family suffered through those meatballs one night each week for years, maybe even until her sister left for college.

To Suzette, beer still tasted disgusting, so she held the cup, pretended to sip it, and listened to the guys tell sailing stories. They popped the tops off of countless bottles as the beer in her own cup grew warmer, eventually matching the temperature of her hands.

Suzette was pretty sure the taste also got worse. One of the other girls noticed she wasn't drinking and pulled a bottle of Boone's Farm Apple wine from the ice in the bathtub.

"Beer is an acquired taste," she said with a wink. "I hate it, too. Try this."

She poured the lukewarm beer down the sink, rinsed the cup, and filled it with wine. Suzette smiled and sipped. It didn't taste a whole lot better, but at least it was sweet.

"Thanks. This is good."

"I'll never understand women," one boy said. "Beer is the nectar of the Gods."

He belched.

Suzette sat on the floor with her back against the hotel room wall. Debbie perched on one of the beds, propped up by pillows, and massaged Robbie's shoulders. Two midshipmen sprawled across the other bed, juggling chips and onion dip. Another shelled peanuts over a trashcan as the night slipped away.

The room felt warmer, and Suzette wasn't sure if it had more to do with the thermostat or the apple wine.

"Wine tastes like... freedom," she decided. Listening to the hum of conversation, her eyelids grew heavy. The next thing she knew, Debbie was shaking her awake. The guys had gone back to their own room, and it was time to get some real sleep. They did, after all, have curfew.

"The starting gun for the Windmill class goes off at eight in the morning," Debbie said, climbing into bed. "We better sleep fast."

They stood at the docks of the St. Petersburg Yacht Club and watched until the sailboats disappeared on the horizon. Slowly, the girls walked back to the parking lot.

"Hey, who's driving the truck?"

"Robbie told me the sailing coach ditched the team 'cause his girlfriend was in town. Some chaperone he turned out to be."

Debbie ran a hand through her hair and thought for a minute.

"The truck can't stay here. The team has to load the boats back on the trailer when they finish the race in Sarasota."

They stared at each other.

"I'm not driving that thing," another girl said.

Suzette's eyes grew wider. She didn't have a license, and even if she did, she didn't think she could drive a truck towing a boat trailer.

"Well, I can't. I don't know how to drive a stick shift."

They turned toward Debbie.

"It's up to you. You're the only one who knows how to drive four-on-the-floor."

True enough, but Debbie was still nervous. This was a much bigger truck, and she would have to drive it over a big bridge. The Sunshine Skyway extended across Tampa Bay, connecting St. Petersburg to Bradenton. Actually, the boats would be sailing directly beneath it, but she had no desire to join them in the water.

"I'm not driving this thing alone."

"I'll ride with you," Suzette offered.

Their bags already were loaded into another station wagon, so they jumped in the crew truck and headed south.

As it climbed the bridge's gentle arch, the pickup truck caught a sudden gust of wind, and Debbie fought with the steering wheel as she tried not to change lanes.

Suzette's heart raced as the palms of her hands started sweating. She began feeling light-headed and had trouble breathing. From the passenger seat, it looked as though Debbie might lose control of the truck and veer off the bridge into the bay. The railing was so close, she could reach out and touch it.

Debbie looked over and sensed the other girl's panic but kept a death grip on the steering wheel.

"Hey, don't worry. I'm a good driver. Just look straight ahead. We're already more than halfway across the bridge."

Suzette glanced out her window and noticed there wasn't even a breakdown lane to pull into in case of an emergency.

As they started to descend, the wind died down.

"With this breeze, the guys should be flying across the water," Suzette said nervously trying to focus on something outside the truck.

Debbie nodded and laughed.

"Depends on how fast they drink the beer in the coolers."

When she could relax enough to think about anything other than her own imminent death, Suzette asked Debbie a question.

"How did you get to know the guys at the academy? I mean, I live there, so I kind of fall over them every day, even if I don't want to. But you...."

She let her words hang in the air.

"They're a lot nicer than the locals in Sanford," she said simply. "The guys at the academy don't judge you. For example, I hang out with a really cool girl at school, but her parents wouldn't let her come to my house because they said they didn't know my family. Can you believe it? I mean, my dad was in the military, and we haven't lived here very long. At least the midshipmen come from someplace else, too. We have that in common."

Suzette understood. Every three years, she had been the outsider, the one looking in. She winced when she heard that Debbie had endured it, too. She felt a familiar ache in the pit of her stomach that she knew had nothing to do with hunger.

CHAPTER 23
Gangway

The academy employed a driver's education instructor affectionately known as "Safeway Jane." She arrived in the afternoon behind the wheel of a large sedan with "Driving School" signs plastered to its doors. Two or three midshipmen at a time accompanied her on local roads and interstate highways.

Suzette figured it would be easier for her to take driving lessons from home, rather than her own high school forty-five minutes away. Her parents figured their insurance rates would drop significantly if she completed any course. Luckily, Safeway Jane agreed to add the Captain's daughter to her schedule of midshipmen.

Suzette's first driving lesson occurred one Saturday morning. She walked out with her mother to meet the instructor and was surprised to see Big Mac (one of her mother's favorite midshipmen) sitting in the back seat of the car. He waved.

"I never got around to taking driver's education and getting my license over the summer."

She felt better. Big Mac would be easy to drive with. He was probably more afraid of looking stupid than she was.

"Okay, cool. I'll try not to hit anything while you're a passenger."

"Thanks. I'll do the same." He grinned.

Their instructor chatted constantly in the car, and she never seemed to watch the road. At first, she took them to a large parking lot and slid into the passenger side of the car.

"Adjust the seat so you can reach all the controls. Okay, now adjust the inside and outside rearview mirrors. You should not have to lean forward or backward to see out of them."

Suzette and Big Mac took turns getting the feel of pressing the accelerator as well as the brake pedal. The following week, they progressed to driving on local streets. It wasn't very hard, since the speed limit never exceeded thirty-five miles per hour.

Big Mac was behind the wheel when Safeway Jane ordered him to the Interstate 4 entrance ramp.

"You've got to accelerate to seventy miles per hour and merge into traffic. Remember to yield the right-of-way to traffic on the expressway. You cannot always count on other drivers moving over to give you room to enter. Once you're on the expressway, drive with the flow of traffic. Driving too slowly can be just as dangerous as driving too fast."

Suzette clenched her fists in the back seat and checked her seat belt.

"I'm glad you're doing this first."

He laughed nervously.

"Yeah, take notes back there."

Safeway Jane glanced up and told Big Mac to get into the right lane. He put on the turn signal, checked his mirrors, and changed lanes.

"I guess you didn't notice the sign back there that said 'Merge Left. Right Lane ends 500 feet.' In order to obtain a Florida Driver's License, you must be able to identify Florida road signs and know what they mean."

"Uh, no ma'am."

"Driver's Education teaches the importance of road awareness and traffic safety for first-time drivers like you two."

They exited in Daytona Beach, and Safeway Jane directed Big Mac to a drive-in restaurant. Coincidentally, Suzette's stomach had just begun to growl as they ordered burgers and fries and settled on a picnic table outside.

"Once you complete your Florida behind-the-wheel training requirement and gain enough driving skills and experience, you can schedule your DMV driving test. It's important to practice the driving maneuvers and techniques you'll be evaluated on during your driving test, like three-point turns and parallel parking. You both are lucky there are a lot of quiet streets around the academy."

"Saturday afternoon would be a good time. Nothing goes on over the weekend."

They finished eating, and Suzette took her place behind the wheel. It was her turn to drive home. They were headed back to the Interstate when Safeway Jane abruptly told her to turn left.

Suzette did but hit the brakes when she noticed a moving vehicle heading directly toward her.

"Generally, the 'One Way' sign means you may travel only in the direction of the arrow, but you didn't see the sign. You just did what someone in your car asked you to do. Always remember to follow the signs, Suzette, not your friends."

Point made.

CHAPTER 24
Scuttlebutt

Parent's Day was held each year on the day before Spring Break began. It was the one time during the school year that parents had the opportunity to observe the daily routine of their sons at the academy. The program consisted of classroom visits throughout the day by parents, a Dad's Golf Tournament at a neighboring country club, a reception, and, finally, a buffet dinner on the Mess Deck.

To prepare for the festivities, semaphore flags were strung across the Quarterdeck before the parents arrived. Suzette watched one midshipman climb down from a ladder after helping the school maintenance man hang flags. She had heard the boy brag about his father, a merchant marine, who had taken his family on many trips throughout the world.

The Captain stopped suddenly and stared at the flags hanging just below the ceiling. He beckoned the maintenance man over.

"They look pretty good up there, don't they sir?" the man asked, wiping his hands.

"Yes, but you need to take them down," the Captain said. Seeing the man's puzzled expression, he explained, "The flags spell H-E-L-L-O S-U-C-K-E-R-S."

One New York couple looked forward to their Parent's Day visit to the academy every year. They loved escaping from the cold and spending a week in Florida. Their only son was the apple of his mother's eye—and gay. Their car pulled under the portico in front of the academy as they spotted Mr. Penn, one of their son's favorite teachers.

Mr. Penn, smiling, accepted her embrace and shook her husband's hand as they entered the building.

"I hope our son is making progress," the man said. "I used to take him to football games, but he was bored. Said he'd rather shop with his mom."

"He's a bright boy," Mr. Penn responded, remembering him perched on a desk in the classroom during an afternoon detention.

"Just to watch Tim Russell take a shower is worth extra reports and a hundred demerits," the boy had whispered, dreamily.

Suzette liked the kid. He was funny, flamboyant, and one of the few guys who didn't seem to mind living at the academy. She ran into him sometimes after cheerleading practice in the gym.

"How do you do it..., fit in here, I mean?" Suzette asked once.

"Well, I like sunshine and palm trees," he answered, grinning. "The lake is certainly prettier than the subways in New York City.

"My father told me he was sending me to a military boarding school 'to make a man out of me'," he continued, sobering. "What does that mean, exactly? I have no clue. I feel like a man, not a homosexual. I don't play the piano or dress like Liberace. I certainly don't want to be a hairdresser when I graduate. I just want a normal life.

"Ironically, Alexander the Great, the most brilliant military strategist in history, had a gay lover," he added. "Maybe I should bring that bit of trivia up in naval history class. What do you think?"

"A brilliant tactic," Suzette said, nodding.

The boy told her about The Sacred Band of Thebes, a troop of soldiers—hand-picked by the Theban commander Gorgidas—consisting of 150 pairs of male lovers which formed the elite force of the Theban army in the fourth century B.C.

"I can survive here," he told Suzette confidently. "My roommate is cool with things. After graduation, I'll probably head back home to New York and go to a liberal arts college. This crazy place might even keep me safe and out of jail. I mean, New York State still has laws on the books that make homosexuality a criminal offense."

"Really?" Suzette gasped.

"Yeah, I know. Ridiculous, right? Kinda' makes this place look better, doesn't it?"

"Coach is really sweet and a very funny guy."

Michelle applied mascara as Suzette stretched out across her sister's bed.

"I don't see him much, outside of football games. He usually just talks to dad."

Michelle had arrived the night before, happy to escape the snow in Massachusetts for Spring Break in Florida. She planned to apply for a summer job at Walt Disney World while she was in town, and she liked having the funny football coach around to date during her visit.

"We're going to hear his friend's band play at a club in downtown Orlando."

She paused and blinked.

"I don't remember the last time I had a date. Most of the people in my fashion design classes are women, and I work in a fabric store on the weekends. That's generally not a great place to pick up guys. Living with Nana and Grampa kind of eliminates meeting eligible bachelors, too. Everybody in their neighborhood is so old."

Suzette laughed. "Yeah, you're kind of stuck when it comes to the dating department."

"It's nice when I get here because the coach does all the planning. I don't know where to go for fun in Florida, but he does, and he seems so thrilled to have me go with him."

"Think about it, Miss Popularity. Where is a football coach going to meet women? He teaches at a boys' boarding school, and my God, he actually lives there, too. He's stuck in the same boat you are."

Michelle finished her makeup and nodded.

"I guess you're right. I hadn't thought about it like that."

It had been easy for her to date a lot when she attended a big university but harder at a small art school. When she was at home, she shopped for groceries and cooked dinner for her grandparents, who were in their early eighties. She didn't mind—she enjoyed cooking, but it didn't leave much time for a social life.

The doorbell rang, and Suzette ran to get it. The coach stood, grinning, with a bouquet of flowers in his hand.

"Hi, squirt. Is your sister ready?"

Michelle beamed like she was seeing the Holy Grail as Mom appeared in the hallway.

"Oh, those flowers are lovely! I'm sure we have a vase in the kitchen. Suzette, will you check?"

As she rifled through the cabinets, Suzette gave the guy credit for the flower delivery. For a football coach, he certainly figured out how to win over all of the LeBlanc women.

$\updownarrow$

"How does the guy get to skip haircuts?" The Menacer lamented to Suzette one Saturday afternoon. Her mother had drafted the kid to help install curtain rods in the apartment and invited him to stay for lunch.

"Thanks again for helping me with my college application, Mrs. LeBlanc," he said earnestly. "I don't think I could've finished it in time without you."

"No problem." Mom looked pleased as she put a ham sandwich in front of him. Skipper sat patiently beside his chair, waiting for a handout.

The Captain headed to the golf course every Saturday, and his absence gave Suzette the chance to hang out with guys at home. Midshipmen felt more relaxed when her father wasn't watching them.

"I sit behind this guy in Naval History class, and I can barely see the board. Since when are midshipmen allowed to wear long afros?"

"Uh, the guy has the only afro in the school since he's the only black student, right?" Suzette asked.

"Still doesn't mean he can grow his hair longer than everyone else," The Menacer replied, helping himself to a bag of potato chips. "The rest of us get demerits and extra duty for skipping haircuts. I think it's time for a lesson in grooming."

Later that afternoon, the midshipman stopped into a drug store, carried a bottle of Nair to the shampoo aisle, opened it, and sniffed. At least it was a creamy color, just like Afro Sheen. Maybe in a steam-filled shower, the guy wouldn't notice the difference.

It took longer than he thought it would, but the Menacer emptied the contents of the shampoo bottle into his toilet and slowly substituted the liquid hair remover.

He watched the guy for a few days and decided the best time to make the switch was during athletics in the afternoon. Fortunately, he had collected keys to most of the locks in the building, so he never had a problem with a door. Quickly, he snatched a bottle of shampoo from the shower and replaced it with the one he'd carried in under his uniform shirt.

With a spring in his step, The Menacer hummed all the way back to his own room.

"Patience is the leading characteristic of great minds," he said, hiding the ring of spare keys under his mattress.

A few days later in Naval History class, he spotted it: A patch of hair had broken off on the top of the other boy's head, leaving a gap.

The Menacer could barely stifle a grin. He still had to lean over one side of his desk to see the board, but he suspected it wouldn't be for much longer.

True enough, by the end of the week, the afro was considerably shorter and trimmed to an even length all around. The missing hunk was no longer noticeable.

Rules apply to everyone, he reasoned. He remembered reading a quote from Benjamin Franklin, who asked himself each morning, "What good shall I do today?"

He felt certain that Mr. Franklin would applaud his choice.

CHAPTER 25
The Bulkhead

H er parents never missed Sunday Mass.
Suzette felt like she should get a reprieve since she attended services at least once a week at Our Lady of Perpetual Guilt—twice, if a "holy day of obligation" occurred.

In fairness, she should be able to skip Sunday services, but where is it written that life is fair? Her father had been an altar server as a boy, and her mother graduated from parochial school.

Suzette clearly suffered for it.

It's not that she didn't have faith. She did. Anyone who ever sat through biology or chemistry midterms understood the power of prayer.

She just wasn't sure her eternal salvation depended upon the Sunday celebration of a ritual dating back to the first century.

Her mother invited Big Mac and his younger brother to join the family for Mass and a bite of lunch afterwards. The local Catholic Church looked pretty on the outside—pale stucco with a red tile roof like the academy, but inside, the place reeked of mildew, an odor of decay that even burning incense couldn't mask. Surrounded by ancient oak trees draped in Spanish moss, the church was dark and gloomy.

Suzette thought that moss looked pretty in pictures and at a distance, sort of like wispy, gray cotton candy, but in her hand, it wasn't soft at all, just curved stems with heavily scaled leaves that early Florida settlers used to stuff inside their mattresses. Waiting for the bus one afternoon, Julie pointed out that Spanish moss sheltered a number of creatures, including jumping spiders and three species of bats. Suzette wondered if those ever made it into old mattresses, too.

When they went to church on the Navy base, it was hilarious for Suzette to see young sailors—who were not much older than the academy midshipmen—become dazzled by the abundance of gold braid on the boys' uniform hats and shoulder boards. The sailors frequently stopped and saluted the high school guys. Suzette understood the confusion because all the bling looked the same to her, too.

The first time it happened, Mike and his brother kind of froze. They weren't actual naval officers and shouldn't be saluted. However, the Captain reassured them.

"Go ahead and return their salute. These guys are taught to respect officers, and at a glance, they can't tell the difference in your uniform. So, don't be rude, go ahead and enjoy the attention."

He winked. "I don't have a problem with it."

Suzette liked the little white chapel on the base because it was cozy—there weren't many pews—and it was always bright inside. She also wasn't a fan of large church choirs (where at least one member always seemed to sing off-key), and this place had a lone organist. She had heard her fair share of Catholic Church choirs.

When the music started, the congregation stood to greet the priest. Instead, they watched a guy who looked like Arnold Palmer walk down the center aisle. Dressed in a golf shirt and slacks, the man looked as though he had just dropped his bag of clubs at the front door.

"How many times have you looked at a person and initially misjudged their intelligence or personality?" he asked, standing at the altar.

"Appearances are deceptive. How we may look to someone and how we actually are may be totally different. First impressions rarely contain the whole truth, and we must remember that."

He slipped into a long, white, liturgical gown as he spoke.

"Have you been a victim of such judgment? Or have you been a perpetrator of it? We form opinions based on superficialities. It's up to us to change those opinions based on a more objective and rational viewpoint."

It turned out to be a pretty good sermon, Suzette thought, with a terrific ending.

"I want you to remember this: Life's greatest gifts rarely are wrapped the way you expected."

As they walked outside into the sunshine, Suzette considered the priest's message. It was true. Appearances can be deceiving. The less you worry about what other people think of you, the less complicated your life will be. Then she grinned at the flurry of salutes from sailors that began when the academy midshipmen passed by.

Okay, God, in this case, it really does matter what you look like on the outside, she thought, but she saw the pride on her friends' faces as they returned those salutes, and it kind of made up for their unintentional deception. This particular morning, they were surrounded by people who respected the uniforms rather than ridiculing them.

In truth, she believed the boys beneath all of the gold braid deserved it, too.

CHAPTER 26
Bow Thrusters

"We've had a very generous offer from the man who runs the school laundry service," the Captain said, sitting down at the dinner table.

"Really? I can't imagine what." Mom raised an eyebrow.

"He owns a house on New Smyrna Beach. Please pass me the salad."

Suzette stopped chewing.

"Do you mean, we could stay at the beach for a weekend?"

"For free?" her mother added.

"The answer to both of you is yes. He said he rarely uses it, and we are welcome to go whenever we want to."

Suzette was delighted.

"That sounds like fun and very kind of him."

"Well, the school gives him a lot of business."

"Maybe some of the boys, like Big Mac, would like to join us. Do you know how big the place is?" Mom asked.

"He mentioned two bedrooms with a sleeping loft upstairs. Actually, it might be nice to treat the kids on my staff to a trip to the beach."

Suzette was surprised to hear him say this. How could her father hide his drinking from midshipmen if they were staying in a beach house together? Could he stop for the weekend?

"We could bring groceries and do our own cooking to keep the costs down," Mom added. "I've seen how much food these teenage boys can eat. Hot dogs, hamburgers, and pasta will go a long way."

Since her sister left for college three years ago, Suzette had traveled alone with her parents, but having guys her age along would make it more fun. By the time Friday afternoon arrived, she was excited to get to the beach house. Before she left for school, she'd packed a tote bag with a couple of bikinis, T-shirts, and shorts. She figured she could sleep in the T-shirts and shorts and wear them to walk on the beach. She certainly wouldn't wear any flimsy nightgowns with midshipmen around. How embarrassing.

The trunk of the Impala was packed with groceries and a cooler when they left the academy late in the afternoon. They drove, watching the high-rise beach condos and T-shirt shops gradually disappear from the sides of the road.

"We must be getting close," the Captain muttered, eyeing some house numbers, but he missed a turn off Atlantic Avenue and drove to the end of the highway. Suzette stared at a large sign, "Canaveral National Seashore, US National Park Service." A guard gate provided access from six a.m. to six p.m. for an entry fee of five dollars per car or motorcycle.

"Maybe we'll come back here and explore." Mom was intrigued.

Big Mac knew that the park was sandwiched between the Atlantic Ocean and the Mosquito Lagoon. That meant there were lots of beaches there, along with a brackish water estuary.

"We'd need plenty of sunscreen, bug spray, sunglasses, hats, bottles of water, and shoes that could handle the beach sand or trail," he said.

"No thanks," Suzette said. "I'm thinking a lounge chair beside the deep blue ocean sounds better."

Minutes later, the car parked in front of a wooden A-frame house. The inside looked plain, but Suzette figured the vinyl floors would make sweeping out any sand they tracked in very easy. Sliding glass doors along the back wall were covered in salt spray that blocked the view. They opened onto a concrete patio facing sand dunes covered in sea grasses.

Suzette walked through a narrow passage between the dunes and gasped: she stood fifty feet from the Atlantic Ocean, its waves crashing on the beach in front of her.

"Nice and close to the water," Mom said, standing behind her. "And I don't think cars are allowed to drive on this end of the beach."

After the groceries were unloaded and their bags stowed, the group changed into swimsuits and headed out to the water. Suzette spread a towel over the hot sand and stretched out.

"Don't get burned."

Mom was very cautious. She generally sat under a beach umbrella wearing a hat and cover-up because her pale, freckled skin had suffered serious sunburns throughout her lifetime.

The sound of the waves—accompanied by screeching seagulls overhead—lulled Suzette to sleep. When she woke, she sat up and spotted her father and the guys wading in waist-deep water. The wind blew their voices towards her, and she listened.

"You need to pick the right wave. Stick to one that's less than four feet high—nothing higher."

Her father was stroking toward the shore to catch a wave, with the boys right behind him. Suddenly, in the foam, their head and shoulders popped up, and their chests became planing surfaces. In effect, their bodies became surfboards.

"It's more of an art than a sport," the Captain said. "This is pure communication with the ocean. I used to do it off the coast of Cape Cod."

Big Mac was panting.

She watched them try again, swimming like mad toward shore, only to start sinking and turning underwater summersaults. The trio stood, sputtering, on shore.

"You want to body surf in waves that break at an angle, from top to bottom, instead of crashing down all at once," the Captain suggested. "I've seen large, crashing waves close to shore break bones."

Later, after exhaustion set in, the guys stood under an outdoor shower while Suzette and her mother headed for the indoor bathroom. She loved the way she felt after washing off salt spray, so warm and relaxed.

"Citronella oil is a natural, plant-based insect repellent," her mother said, as she lit candles on the wooden picnic table. "It's non-toxic and supposedly poses no health risks."

"Unless you are a mosquito," Suzette interjected.

A warm breeze blew off the ocean as the smell of hamburgers rose from the barbecue grill.

"A day at the beach always makes me sleepy," she said to no one in particular.

"Looked like you were sleeping most of the afternoon." Big Mac laughed. "Have a Coke. That should keep you awake."

Her arms and legs glowed slightly pink, and her finger left an imprint on her arm whenever she touched it.

"Good thing you used sunscreen." Big Mac nodded at her, and she noticed the bridge of his own nose looked bright red.

"Seems like food always tastes better at the beach," Suzette said as she grabbed a handful of pretzel sticks.

"Must be the salt air." The Captain placed a large pot of baked beans on the grill. Suzette was surprised to see her father clearly enjoying himself without a drink in his hand.

"I remember Mom packing jelly sandwiches for me when we used to go to Cape Cod. I could never figure out why they were always crunchy at the beach, but not at home."

"Not the brightest crayon in the box, were you?" Big Mac said.

Everyone started laughing, and soon, Suzette was laughing too. They tossed their paper plates into a trash bag and tied it shut before settling into Adirondack chairs. The back of each chair was angled, tilting their heads toward the sky. With Skipper curled in her lap, Suzette had to admit, life felt pretty good.

"You can really tell we're nowhere near the city," the Captain said. "There's no light pollution to block our view of the stars."

Her opinion of Florida was definitely improving.

The battalion commander drummed his fingers on a cafeteria table. Graduation was looming, and no senior prank had occurred.

The graduating class considered the usual ones that involved a fountain; dye the water, or fill it with bubble bath. The naval academy didn't have a fountain, but it did have a swimming pool. Bill was concerned about causing any permanent damage to it. The prank needed to leave a lasting impression without getting anyone expelled before they could graduate.

"It has to be memorable, something worth talking about at our class reunions," Tim said.

"The more people who are in on it, the better the chance that we'll get busted," another cautioned.

"Who's the faculty member on duty tonight?"

"The Captain, I think."

The Menacer smiled.

"Gentlemen, there'll be no need to hit the workout room tomorrow. You'll get your exercise tonight."

A small group walked to the Quarterdeck, and the battalion commander nodded toward the Volkswagen Beetle the Captain had recently purchased for his wife. The car was parked in front of the school.

"I think the ship's bell needs company, don't you?"

In the center of the Quarterdeck, a large, brass bell hung suspended in a wooden frame. It stood on a red carpet, emblazoned with the school crest. The area was considered sacred ground, and midshipmen weren't allowed to walk on it, under penalty of demerits. The only exception was a sporting victory. Winning teams were allowed to ring the bell.

A few faces grew pale.

"On the red carpet? They'll kill us."

"Hey, there are plastic tarps in the boat shed. I'll grab one."

"Excellent idea. One can't be too careful with the school crest."

They agreed to meet in the shadows under the portico after Taps was blown and "Lights Out" was called.

Then, ten strong but silent pairs of hands lifted the VW up the Spanish tile steps in front of the school. They paused to rest while a single midshipman kept watch on the central staircase, in case the Captain finished his rounds early.

Suzette flipped off her bathroom light and headed for bed. The blinds were open in the window beside her bed, and as she walked past, a movement outside caught her eye. She squinted, then groped on the nightstand to find her glasses and looked again. It appeared that either a baby elephant or a small car was on the front steps to the school. She pulled up the blinds and could see students silhouetted in the dim light.

154

"Oh, my God," she whispered.

She turned, preparing to run to her parents' room and then stopped. She couldn't remember if her father had been drinking earlier, but sober or not, he'd be angry at being awakened in the middle of the night for a student prank.

"Then what?" she asked herself aloud. "Somebody will get expelled, and it will be my fault."

She looked out the window again. The car was gone, probably inside the building, so she dropped the blinds and climbed into bed.

The car cleared the double-entry doors easily and with a few final grunts, it was lowered beside the bell.

A round of high-fives and a quick photo followed before the pranksters ran to the fire escapes, returning to their rooms, undetected. Most of them were sleeping soundly by two o'clock the next morning when the Captain's voice blared from speakers above deck.

"All companies report to the Quarterdeck immediately. Repeat. All companies report to the Quarterdeck immediately."

Midshipmen staggered down the stairs in their pajamas, gym shorts, and T-shirts.

"Gentlemen, I need to know who did this," he bellowed. "Come forward, and do the honorable thing."

The younger boys could hardly believe what they saw on the Quarterdeck. They rubbed their eyes and grinned, pointing to the compact car.

The corners of The Menacer's mouth twitched upward, but he didn't smile or glance at his co-conspirators. Apart from the din of excited conversation among the younger kids, no one stepped forward to acknowledge the crime.

The battalion commander approached the Captain.

"Sir, with your permission, I'm sure I can find several midshipmen to assist me in returning your car to the parking lot."

The Captain nodded, grimly.

"Thank you, sir. I would greatly appreciate that. Maybe it's time for me to buy a Cadillac for my wife."

CHAPTER 27
Sea Trial

The Captain emerged from his office to discover his wife and his secretary deep in conversation. He glanced at his watch.

"Would you ladies care to join me for lunch on the Mess Deck? Do you have plans?"

"Absolutely not. What are they serving?" Bunny Phillips locked her desk drawer and picked up her purse.

"Hamburgers, I think," the Captain said, holding the swinging door that led to the Quarterdeck for the women.

"Sure beats cooking," his wife added.

They walked through the cafeteria line—though the commandant's wife stopped for a few hugs—and settled at a table overlooking Lake Monroe. The spot usually was reserved for faculty and staff members who enjoyed the waterfront view more than midshipmen.

The Captain walked to the center of the room.

"Gentlemen, I have an announcement to make."

The clanking sound of spoons in baked beans stopped.

"I've just hung up the phone from the commanding officer of the U.S.S. Saratoga, an aircraft carrier currently docked at the Naval Station in Mayport. That is a major United States Navy base in Jacksonville, Florida. Sanford Naval Academy students have been invited aboard to tour the ship during a Friends & Family Day Cruise, next Thursday. It is an opportunity for you to see up close what the U.S. Navy does each day. You will observe operations at sea, catapult launches, and aircraft breaking the sound barrier. We are fortunate that the commanding officer's son is a student here. This will be an experience you'll never forget."

Loud cheering only surpassed the sound of clapping hands.

"I think they like the idea," the Captain said, grinning.

The following week, midshipmen boarded school buses at five in the morning.

Hardly awake—but wearing their dress uniforms—boys dozed in the darkness as the buses chugged north on Interstate 95. Suzette and her mother shared a seat in the front of one bus. When she woke up, Suzette noticed the bus was parked next to a gray building. She rubbed her eyes.

"How much longer until we get there?"

"We are there," her mother answered. "Look up."

Suzette looked out of the bus window and followed the gray building toward the sky. It was the flight deck of the U.S.S. Saratoga, and the sight of it so close by nearly took her breath away.

Following the midshipmen aboard, Suzette noticed that with each step, the ship appeared to rise in the water to meet her foot.

She was excited to be among the crew's friends and family members as they experienced, firsthand, how the Saratoga's sailors keep the carrier at sea and operational. After observing the underway process, eating a catered lunch of Florida grouper and grilled vegetables—the cook on board, she learned, took every advantage when the ship was docked to get local ingredients— the naval academy group gathered with the rest of the guests on the flight deck for a demonstration of the ship's air and weapons power performed by Fighter Squadrons and Saratoga's Weapons Department.

Suzette watched the aircraft landing pattern, touch-and-go landings, arrested landings, catapult launches, and aircraft breaking the sound barrier during the demonstration. She realized what life was like for her father when he served on an aircraft carrier. Running a boys' boarding school definitely seemed boring by comparison.

Most of the midshipmen were delighted by their freedom to wander the ship. Occasionally, armed marines would stop them and politely say, "Sorry, sir. This is a restricted area."

But, generally, they could explore the entire vessel throughout the day.

"I'm fairly certain the air power demonstration is going to be the thing that these boys will talk about the most," said the Captain, shaking hands with the Family Day Cruise Coordinator. "It's as close as they'll come to being an aviation boatswain's mate without joining the Navy."

As they climbed aboard the bus at the end of the day, many boys' ears were still ringing from the deafening noise of the jets. Suzette turned to her mother. "That was an amazing air show. When they said that freedom is loud, they weren't exaggerating."

The bell rang, and as the midshipmen filed out of his classroom, Mr. Penn called to two of them.

"Mr. Moore, Mr. McGrath, I need a few minutes of your time."

Bill and Big Mac nodded as they approached his desk.

"I have a situation that could really use your help. My sister has been having problems with her landlord, a lecherous, old guy. Unfortunately, he just evicted her."

"Sorry to hear that, sir."

"She plans to move out on Saturday morning, but she's really afraid this guy might cause some trouble. I offered to help, but she tells me he has two, rather large, redneck sons who act as his goon squad. I told her I could probably round up a little extra muscle to help load her trailer and to look menacing, if it comes to that. You guys came to mind. Are you up for it?"

"Of course, sir. What time do you need us?"

"I can swing by the school and pick you up around nine o'clock. I appreciate it; I really do. And no uniforms, okay? Just wear jeans and t-shirts with no SNA logos. Let's keep things anonymous."

They grinned.

"I'll get Robbie to help."

"I can get another midshipman, too," added Big Mac. "No problem."

Saturday morning, the group got out of Mr. Penn's car in front of an old, wooden house that sagged atop its cinderblock foundation. Spider webs clung to paint that was peeling off ancient wood siding. A dirt yard stood where grass was supposed to grow and—apart from termites—it was difficult to imagine anything could live there.

Tree roots beneath the concrete driveway had grown large enough to break the driveway into chunks. Still, a rental truck had managed to back in, and a pretty young woman was carrying a box out of the house. They walked to the broken front steps and introduced themselves before hoisting pieces of furniture onto the truck.

"At least we didn't have any packing to do," said Big Mac, drinking a can of soda on the porch. "She already did it all, and there's really not too much to move."

As he dropped the empty can back into a cooler, he noticed a pickup truck pulling up to the curb.

"Uh, Mr. Penn, we've got company."

The midshipmen finished stacking boxes in the truck and joined Big Mac on the porch. Robbie paused in the front doorway and put the lamp down. Bill crossed his arms and leaned against the porch railing.

The group unconsciously fell into military formation, a kind of protective phalanx around the entrance to the dilapidated house. Mr. Penn and his sister walked toward the men, who never came closer than the curb.

"Should we move forward if anyone starts screaming or swinging?" Tim asked, quietly.

"Give it time," Bill answered. "Nobody's raised their voice, yet."

"We could take those guys," Big Mac interjected. "They don't look very big."

Fortunately, the group didn't have to. Mr. Penn returned to the house looking visibly relieved, and his sister's eyes filled with tears as she thanked each midshipman for coming to help her.

"Guys, I'm grateful," Mr. Penn said, when they were back in the car. "You didn't just help the lady move out; you kept her safe. I owe you dinner."

"Thank you, sir, but we were happy to help. Haven't you read the handbook? 'Honor, duty, and service to others.' We just follow the rules."

CHAPTER 28
Following Seas

"Those colors are very flattering."

Mom cocked her head to one side and looked at Suzette in the mirror. Her daughter had tried on at least ten long dresses, and most of them made her look like Popeye's girlfriend, Olive Oyl—utterly shapeless and straight.

The winner was a blue, green, and violet print that crisscrossed in a halter at her neck and left her shoulders exposed. It wasn't too daring and definitely concealed Suzette's lack of boobs.

Mom loved it.

"Maybe you should ask Bill for a wrist corsage," she suggested. "There's really no place to pin one on your chest or bare shoulders."

Suzette was kind of excited about going to the academy P-R-O-M, which her friend Julie explained was a short form of the word "Promenade," meaning "to walk with pleasure." The battalion commander had asked permission from the Captain to invite her to prom. Like he needed it—her parents were chaperones, for God's sake.

Yet, the whole thing seemed especially intriguing because—like Suzette—none of her freshman friends had ever been to one. At Our Lady of Perpetual Guilt, prom was one of the main events of senior year. It was considered a privilege to attend. Couples—usually both seniors—posed for pictures, went to expensive restaurants recommended by their parents, appeared at the dance for a couple of hours, went to an after party, got drunk, and had sex. The event signified the end of their high school career and dressing in formal attire was supposed to show the world how much they had grown and matured.

Suzette felt like a complete fraud… an underage, extremely appreciative fraud, who needed a lot of makeup *and a padded bra* to get through the door.

She was totally thrilled.

Several of the girls on the cheerleading squad scheduled salon appointments to have their hair done up in curls or French twists.

"Your hair is one of your best features," Mom said. "Wear it down, and curl it. You'll look beautiful."

Suzette agreed, figuring it was one less thing she had to worry about. *Cinderella probably felt this way just before her pumpkin turned into a coach,* she thought.

She asked her date for white flowers, either roses or orchids, for her wrist corsage and ordered a white rose boutonnière for his tuxedo lapel. She had no idea what color shirt or tie the guy would be wearing, and she didn't feel comfortable asking about it. It's not like they were a steady couple or anything. It would have been pretty impossible for him to match Suzette's dress, anyway, because the chiffon looked like Monet's water lilies—if Monet had been drunk when he painted them.

It was easy to go to prom with a friend. The battalion commander was safe, and even better, he was hilarious.

Still, a lot of seniors wouldn't make it to their prom because they didn't have dates. The Menacer complained about that fact to Suzette one afternoon after cheerleading practice.

"Even at football and basketball games, you know what we look like to local girls? A sea of gray uniforms with stupid haircuts. We don't have girls in our classes. Where else can we meet anyone?"

Suzette understood. Too often we let the rejections of our past dictate every move we make. However, she was acutely aware that a lack of more suitable candidates allowed her to be invited to the senior prom. And she was grateful.

She knew some of the cheerleaders set guys up with their friends from Sanford High School. However, Suzette couldn't do that because her friends were in the ninth grade and lived too far away. She definitely wasn't a matchmaker.

In spite of his dateless situation, The Menacer neglected to mention that, in lieu of actually attending the prom, he planned to provide some of the evening's entertainment.

"Magnesium reacts violently with many substances, causing fire and an explosion hazard," the chemistry teacher said. "It reacts with acid and water by forming flammable hydrogen gas."

After unlocking the lab and removing some of the magnesium, The Menacer walked downtown to the grocery store during afternoon liberty. There, he spent a fair amount of time reading the ingredients listed on cardboard boxes containing instant breakfast drinks. He bought two, planning a "dress rehearsal" with one.

One evening, after the final notes of "Taps" ended, he punched several holes in one of the boxes and added magnesium to the mix. He headed to Lake Monroe, just out of the rent-a-cop's line of sight, and tossed the box into the water. The moment it hit, the box exploded.

"Well, I'll be damned."

The Menacer was pleased. The show would go on.

On Saturday night, Suzette and her date waited in line with other couples to pose for prom pictures on the massive staircase. She heard rock 'n roll music blaring from the former hotel ballroom, and when she peeked in, she was surprised to see a lead singer with shoulder-length hair wearing a suit and tie. He obviously was making a concession to playing a gig at a boys' military academy. Maybe wearing a suit was even written into his contract.

Her parents stood by the punchbowl chatting with Bunny Phillips and her husband. There never seemed to be a shortage of chaperones at these events because Suzette suspected there was never much else to do in Sanford.

She tried to ignore the adults and danced until the band took a break. Fortunately, the battalion commander was a pretty good dancer.

Sweating—and with their ears ringing—many couples walked out of the French doors that lined one wall of the ballroom and strolled toward the lake in the moonlight. None noticed one, lone midshipman sitting on the seawall (though the boy's roommate and his date stayed on the patio, close to the building.)

Ka-Boom!

A flash of light erupted from the water sending guys and girls running. Above Lake Monroe, a hydrogen cloud formed and floated lazily on a North wind, toward the school.

"What in the hell…?"

The Captain and his wife rushed out to the patio and began frantically waving midshipmen and their dates back into the ballroom. Four sets of glass doors slammed shut just before the clouds of gas wrapped the building in a filmy embrace.

"You don't suppose any of them got their hands on atomic weapons, do you?" Mom murmured quietly.

"I'll check on that," the Captain replied. "In the meantime, I suggest you taste the punch before you drink any of it. We can't be too careful with chemicals around here."

The only benefit of scheduling a ten o'clock dental appointment was skipping her morning classes. As they walked to the car, Suzette and her mother were startled to see the entire battalion standing at attention on the lawn in front of the academy.

"I wonder what's going on," Mom mused. "These boys should be in class."

The Captain spotted them and walked over to the car. He lowered his voice as he leaned into the window.

"The business office is missing hundreds of dollars in cash, and since there was no sign of forced entry, they think someone's got a key. Faculty members are searching the midshipmen's rooms right now, and if they don't find anything upstairs, we'll search the kids themselves."

As they drove away, Suzette spotted a group marching across First Street toward the gym. The boys were about to be escorted—in groups of three—into one of the locker rooms and strip searched.

Just before lunch, Bill Moore left the gym with his roommate. The officers had been the last to be searched, and both were puzzled about the reason why.

"Whatever they're looking for, it must be something big."

Bill felt certain the Captain would share information when he could. He hadn't even objected to being strip searched. Fair is fair; there can be no favoritism among the ranks.

Walking slowly across the street, the battalion commander noticed the black asphalt was now speckled with white spots—like albino freckles. It looked as if a tickertape parade recently passed by.

His roommate spotted them too and paused, momentarily, in the middle of the street. Then he began to laugh.

Joints littered the ground, slipped from midshipmen's pockets en route to the gym.

"Well, one thing is certain. We know the Captain didn't find any drugs."

Faculty members, however, found dozens of keys tied to a string and hidden in The Menacer's box spring beneath his mattress. None opened the door to the business office, and no cash was discovered. Still, bottles of rum, scotch, and bourbon violated the academy rules.

The punishment was simple. The Menacer was going home. He would not be allowed to graduate with his class.

Suzette could see that her father was torn. He knew the boy didn't steal any money from the business office which had been the reason for the search. Still, he had been warned about having alcohol in his room on two previous occasions. Underage drinking was against the rules. No exceptions. It seemed ironic that her father would dismiss some guy for a drinking problem.

School officials also found the number of keys in the kid's possession to be troubling. Though his heart wasn't really in it, the Captain was forced to carry out the dismissal.

The next day, Suzette saw The Menacer sitting in her father's office, obviously humiliated by the fact that his parents were driving from Tampa to pick him up.

"As your life unfolds, you will often realize that many of the times you thought you were being rejected from something good, you were actually being redirected to something better," she heard the Captain say. "In the future, you need to follow the rules and do your best. Things will work out because sometimes, the outcomes you can't change end up changing you and helping you grow to your full potential."

CHAPTER 29
Anchors Aweigh

Suzette leaned into the mirror until her breath nearly fogged it. It's kind of hard to apply mascara when you're near-sighted.

She hummed along with a James Taylor song about seeing a friend again, but her stomach wasn't feeling right. It ached the way it did the first few times she went to slumber parties, not badly enough to take an aspirin, but not really easy to ignore. She couldn't eat breakfast, even if she had the time.

"We should probably leave in twenty minutes." Mom peered around the corner into Suzette's bedroom, her hair in rollers and carrying her teacup. "That looks nice."

Her daughter was wearing a black and white tunic with matching, white, pique hot pants beneath it. Suzette figured it would look nice in pictures, next to midshipmen in dress-white uniforms.

"Dad left early to get organized, but he won't remember to save us good seats at the Civic Auditorium." She disappeared.

A short while later, mother and daughter walked to their car but could barely get the doors open. An enormous Cadillac was parked ridiculously close. The rear trunk stood open, and Suzette could hear a man with a loud New Jersey accent bellow, "My son tells me all about you."

Mr. Penn stood gazing adoringly at a case of Scotch with his name on it. Several families brought gifts to teachers who helped their sons. Suzette remembered hearing Mr. Penn rhapsodize about "Mafia parents" to her parents.

"Those parents back teachers to the hilt," he had said. "They believe in discipline, and they can't do enough for you if you take care of their kid. Whenever there's a disagreement, they take the teacher's side. *'You know more than your teacher? Where's the diploma on the wall? Show me your diploma'.*"

The graduating senior class marched in formation into the auditorium, their white uniforms practically glowing. Graduation speeches always killed Suzette. "Satisfying rewards... blah, blah... success and achievement... blah, blah."

An American Legion Plaque for leadership was presented with a round of applause. Truth be told, the midshipmen were as thrilled to hang up their uniforms and leave the school as most faculty members were to be rid of them.

Sitting next to her mother on a cold metal chair, Suzette barely listened. Instead, she studied the well-dressed crowd seated around her... lots of sparkling jewelry and expensive haircuts. She focused her attention back to the stage in time to see the incoming Battalion Commander—John something—salute Bill Moore.

Then, commencement ended with the lowering of the American flag. Suddenly, sixty white hats flew into the air, and chaos erupted. Suzette turned and stared at the throngs of people—aunts and uncles, brothers and sisters, mothers and fathers—and stepmothers and stepfathers—the invisible families she had heard so little about.

Actually, she had even questioned their existence until now—until they magically appeared to play the role of proud, supportive family, leaving Suzette and her mother hovering nearby, waiting for an introduction or an invitation to join the group. It felt a lot like waiting to be picked for a team in gym class; you don't feel quite good enough.

Who were these people anyway? Where were they when their sons sat at the LeBlanc's kitchen table, agonizing over prom dates and college applications? Cruising the Black Sea?

Suzette's family was their true family. These parents were merely invited *guests*. The hole in her heart grew bigger as she watched the midshipmen's embraces continue. Finally, when she couldn't hold it in any longer, the sadness bubbled up and began streaming down Suzette's face, taking most of her mascara with it.

"I'm afraid I'm not doing very well," Suzette mumbled to someone's older sister as she wiped her eyes.

"You're doing fine," the woman answered in a soothing tone.

Suzette and her parents weren't invited to join any midshipmen and their families for a graduation lunch. Most of the guys probably were delighted to be rid of their commandant, and she couldn't blame them. The celebration ended abruptly and the three drove home to their apartment at the academy in silence. The building seemed like an even bigger shell than usual—as empty and disappointing as finding out the rabbit in your Easter basket was only hollow chocolate.

Suzette looked at herself in the mirror: blackened eyes, blurred lips, and her Clinique blush replaced with pink, orange, and red lipstick smudges from a few of the boys' mothers who had planted kisses on her cheeks. Her head was throbbing, a by-product of crying. She washed her face, hung up her dress, and collapsed on top of the bed, emotionally drained.

She listened to a song about sunny skies weeping because everyone was leaving, while sunny skies stayed behind.

Suzette jerked the 8-track tape out. No more James Taylor today.

She didn't know how long she slept, but she barely heard the knock on the door that woke her.

Slightly disoriented, Suzette opened it slowly. The midshipman standing on the other side was taller than her, and his shiny, brown hair looked a bit long to pass an inspection. But she liked the way his eyes crinkled behind his glasses when he smiled.

"Hi, I'm John Bernegger. Is the Captain available?"

In spite of the day she had, Suzette found herself smiling back. The new battalion commander definitely looked promising....

About The Author

Renee is a former staff writer for The Tampa Tribune newspaper and spent ten years as its architecture critic, winning two communication awards from the American Institute of Architects. Her blog, ReneeWritesNow.wordpress.com, contains a short story, "The Anchor Clankers," from which this manuscript originated. The novel, the first in a series, is based on her life. Yes, she grew up in a boys' naval academy.

In 2011, Renee and her husband moved to Florida, a short drive from her former home, The Sanford Naval Academy. At that time, the building was owned by missionaries, who graciously gave her a tour. Memories flooded back and a book was born.

CPSIA information can be obtained
at www.ICGtesting.com
Printed in the USA
LVOW03s1301170717

541443LV00001B/2/P